CROSS COUNTRY 101

CROSS COUNTRY 101

More than just putting one foot in front of the other as fast as you can.

Dan Martinez

Published by Running Entertainment
www.runningentertainment.com

For information about special discounts for bulk purchases in the
United States by corporations, institutions, other organizations, or
other, please email: running@runningentertainment.com
or write: P.O. Box 10663, Glendale, CA 91209.

Illustrations by **Liang Shan**

Library of Congress Control Number: 2012903304

ISBN-10: 0985181613
ISBN-13: 978-0-9851816-1-1

[1. Cross country-Fiction. 2. Running-Fiction. 3. Identity-Fiction.
4. High school-Fiction. 5. Team sports-Fiction. 6. California-Fiction.]

For Caitlin & Brendan.

First Edition-2012
Printed in the United States of America
10 9 8 7 6 5 4 3 2 1

Acknowledgments

First and foremost, I want to thank Stuart Calderwood for his keen editorial sense and skills in getting the book ready for publication.

I also want to thank, Josephine Dell'Anno who assisted me through the editing process.

And

special thanks to Scott "Scotty" Dugan for his feedback on the original story idea.

CONTENTS

Hundreds of pairs of running shoes are crowded together behind the starting line at the California State Championship Cross Country meet. The shoes are many colors and sizes, but they're all made with an unusual economy of fabric and rubber. The uppers are featherweight nylon. The midsoles are a quarter-inch thick at the heel and decrease in thickness toward the toe—a streamlining that barely allows for cushioning. Tough leather trim holds the shoes together. The thin rubber soles are artfully designed to maintain traction over asphalt, dirt, grass, and mud. These shoes are specifically constructed for speed and nothing else. They are made for racing.

Eric Hunt takes his place among the 189 other runners. Even among these slightly-built boys, he is conspicuously small: five feet, one inch tall and 105 pounds. He has curly black hair and olive skin, and he looks younger than fourteen-years-old. His varsity uniform is white shorts and a white singlet with a screaming eagle printed on the chest, representing his school, Regal High. But he is running for himself. There was a time when he didn't give running a second thought, certainly not as a sport. It was always about running away from the bullies in school, running for your life. He didn't even know he was fast or that he wanted to be faster. He didn't know that running was more than races and medals. He had no motivation for running or any other sport. Sports were discouraging. He was always among the last kids chosen at pick-up games, and the other boys would complain about being stuck with him.

However, he'd been passionate about video games. He stayed up late at night playing, competing hard against his invisible opponents: other online players, his best previous scores, topping the highest scores on the games themselves. He had set his mind to winning this kind of competition, and he had practiced until he excelled.

A shout from the sidelines gets Eric's attention: "Go, Todd!" The name had been meaningless to Eric a couple of months ago. Now, it fires his competitive spirit. Todd Bryce has been the fastest freshman all season long and has the potential to be a state champion. He has also been an incentive for Eric to practice every day, to strive to be the best he can be. This is Eric's last chance of the year to prove himself; to be as good as Todd is, maybe even beat him. He has come to this point since running found him, like destiny, on the first day of school.

Early September

Eric Hunt walks through the city park on his way to Regal High for the first day his freshman year. He's a little nervous, since he doesn't know anyone there—and it's high school, after all. He wonders what the other kids will be like. As one of the smallest kids in his class, he always had some trouble in middle school. He's just had a growth spurt that put him at five-feet-one. Eric is fast, and he's always been able to outrun the bullies. That's what's kept him going. He hopes he won't have to deal with any bullies at Regal. He's heard that high school is different; that students are more mature, more grown-up. He continues through the park, a place he usually avoids. His parents think it's a little dangerous— too many kids hanging out getting high and misbehaving—but it's the shortest way to the school. Eric walks briskly toward a garbage can on the side of the path. He hears a faint sound. As he nears the can, it grows louder. Eric recognizes the sound as a bird chirping, and it's coming from inside the can. He looks inside and sees a pigeon with a bad foot and marks on its wings. Eric gently puts his hands around the bird, lifts it out, and examines it. The bird has wounds like it was hit with pellets or rocks, and other marks that look like cigarette burns.

"C'mon, little pigeon. Don't be afraid," Eric says. The pigeon lies in his hands, shaking. Then, miraculously, it flies away.

"Looks like you're going to make it," Eric says. He smiles as he resumes his trek to school. In another minute he hears voices coming from behind a large shelf of rock: boys laughing, and one boy crying in pain. Eric walks slowly across the grass toward the rock outcropping. An object in the grass catches his attention and he picks it up. It's a large button—oddly, just like the ones on his jacket. There is another cry of pain. Eric puts the button in his pocket. He carefully makes his way between the rocks to a tree. Silently, he climbs the tree's large lower branches to see over the rocks. He peers through leaves and sees two large boys—high school sophomores, maybe juniors—wearing football jerseys. The bigger of the two, clearly the leader, is on the heavy side, with broad shoulders, a large chest, and beefy arms. His smaller sidekick has dark hair. They're laughing and smoking; from the way they pinch the rolled cigarette and pass it back and forth, Eric knows it's weed. On the ground, under the bigger kid's foot, is a small boy, probably Eric's age, wearing a jacket just like Eric's. The big kid has pulled the small boy's undershorts out from his pants and up into a "wedgie." The other kid drops a soda can next to the prone boy's head.

"This is what's gonna happen to you if you tell anyone," the kid with the can warns. He stomps down on the can right near the victim's ear. The bigger kid yanks on the shorts.

"Awwwwh!" the small boy cries out in pain. His tormentors start laughing again.

"Look at him squirm, just like that pigeon," remarks the kid who stomped the can. His buddy takes a drag, then bends down and blows smoke into the trapped kid's face.

"You gettin' high, bro?" the big kid says, laughing. His friend takes a drag, leans into the little kid's face, and blows smoke into his nostrils. He coughs and twists his face away.

"C'mon, get high with us," the big guy says. Suddenly there's a loud cracking sound. The branch Eric is standing on cracks and gives way. The two football players are startled. Instinctively, the big one releases the small kid's shorts and steps off him. The other guy throws down the joint and looks toward the tree. Eric slips to the ground and grabs the tree for support, which

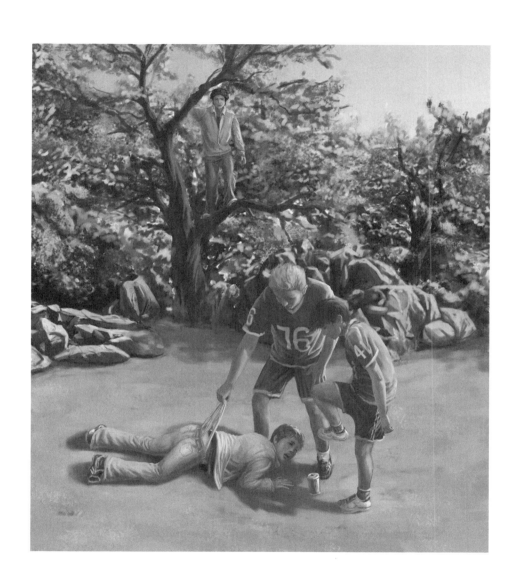

leaves him out in the open, exposed. He lets go of the tree and slips, just missing some rocks and falling onto the grass.

The little kid rolls out, gets up, and runs away. The football players disregard him. They rush over to the tree and approach Eric.

Eric is still on the ground when they arrive. They offer to help him up. Their intimidating size instantly makes Eric uneasy. They help Eric up, and he brushes himself off and starts to walk away.

"Thanks," Eric says.

He keeps walking, keenly aware that the boys are now following him. The few seconds that pass seem to take forever. Finally they catch up to him, one on either side, towering over him as if in a cruel game of "Monkey in the Middle."

"What's up, little guy?" the big one asks.

"Yeah, where you goin' in such a hurry?" the other kid adds.

Eric stares straight ahead. "School. I don't want to be late the first day."

"Which school?"

"Regal."

"You a freshman?"

"Yeah."

The big kid laughs. "You look like you should be in grade school, doesn't he, Crush?"

"Yeah, Beef, you're right," Crush says. "We'd better walk with you. It's not safe."

"Hey, man, you party?" Beef asks.

He doesn't give Eric a chance to reply.

"You know what happens to guys who don't keep their mouth shut?" Beef says, lowering his voice.

Suddenly they grab Eric by the shoulders. Just as quickly, Eric bolts, tearing away from their grasp, leaving them stumbling after him. Eric isn't sure where he's going, but he figures anyplace is safer than an isolated park path devoid of people. As he runs into a clearing, he sees a boy about his size standing near a park bench. As Eric gets closer, he sees that it's the boy with the jacket like his. When the boy notices Eric and the older boys rushing toward him, he takes off as if the older boys are after him, too.

The path ends and Eric emerges into a sunny open field. He runs straight for the main road, which is busy with morning traffic. He manages to lose the boy called Crush, but the one called Beef keeps coming, refusing to give up. The giant puts on speed and, with a desperate last effort, dives to grab him. Eric speeds up yet again, eluding the jock's grasp. The big kid falls face-first onto the grass.

Without slowing down, Eric dashes across the field and catches up to the small kid. He glances back to see Beef sitting up, spitting and wiping grass off his face, with Crush walking up to him and laughing. When they're a safe distance away, Eric comes to a stop with the small kid, who's about five feet tall with brown hair, and they both catch their breath. As traffic speeds past them, they begin to walk.

"My name's Paul Tate," the boy says.

"Eric Hunt. I'm a freshman."

"I'm a freshman, too," says Paul.

"Nice jacket."

"Hey, yeah, I like yours, too. You heading to Regal?"

"Yep."

"Me, too. Wow, you sure can run! I wish I was that fast."

The traffic light turns red and they cross the street.

"I can run pretty far," Paul goes on, "but I can't sprint. If I'd had a bigger head start they wouldn't have caught me. Look at this." He lifts his jacket and shirt to reveal a torn length of his underwear's waistband hanging out of his pants. "They're ruined."

"I saw that," Eric says.

"Man, thanks!" Paul exclaims. "You gave me just enough time to get out of there. I'm glad you got away, too. You're pretty fast," he mutters, still in awe.

Eric laughs. "I've been running away from creeps like that all my life."

At the entrance to the school, they check to make sure the bullies haven't followed them. School busses unload students, and Eric and Paul are surrounded by a flurry of voices and movement. They join the stream of teenagers walking toward the entrance and pass a large digital sign that reads WELCOME BACK, STUDENTS. Beside it is a posting for football tryouts.

"My dad wants me to go out for football," Eric says. "I managed to avoid the pre-season workouts in the summer, but I can't put it off any more, now that school's started."

"Why would you play at all, with jerks like that on the team?" Paul says. "They'll pulverize you. You should go out for cross country."

"Cross country? What's that?"

"It's running, like what you just did—except longer. Five thousand meters. That's three-point-one miles over grass and hills, only you get your picture taken for it. I got my picture in this national magazine from the summer. Wanna see?"

Eric shrugs. "Sure."

Paul unbuttons his jacket and digs into a pocket. Eric notices that a button's missing near the middle. Remembering the button he'd found in the park, he fishes it out.

"I found this," Eric says.

"My button! Awesome! Those jerks yanked it off when they grabbed me. Thanks."

Paul puts the button in his pocket and takes out a folded page that's been ripped from a magazine. In the center of the article is a large photograph of runners standing on a starting line. Paul is closest to the camera, in a racing uniform. He's the shortest of the group.

Eric smiles. "That's pretty cool."

The Regal High physical education teacher and cross country coach, Ken Morris, strides past the front-desk area of the athletic director's office. In his mid-thirties, lean and tan, wearing a T-shirt and sweatpants, he knocks on the door and enters. Edward Stone, a man in his late forties, sits behind the desk looking over the school's sports program budget, looks up and puts the papers down.

"You wanted to see me, Ed?" Coach Morris asks. Ed stands up and shakes his hand.

"Hi, Ken, have a seat," Ed says. The coach sits, nervous. Something is up.

"This is a very tough decision but one I feel I have to make. It's the damn economy, nothing else," Ed says. He takes a deep breath and blurts out, "Let me get to the point, Ken. This season looks like it's going to be the last for the cross country team. I can't justify the cost for a program that doesn't have enough participants. How do you expect to be competitive?"

"But Ed, think of the kids that do run—they're good," Morris replies. "Remember when I came here? You couldn't even get kids to run. Now I finally pulled a team together, and I know it's taking a while, but we're getting up to speed. These things take time."

"You didn't have enough kids for a team last year. This year it looks like you have the bare minimum. This is very hard, but I have to cut costs in the athletic department, and cross country just doesn't produce. Maybe if you'd gotten to State, things would be different."

"I got Vance to State. He was third at the state meet, the fastest junior."

"That was track. Where was he in cross country?"

"He got injured last fall," Coach says. "He's fine now and running better than ever. Come on. How many times does a football player get injured a year?"

Ed shakes his head.

"And Barry. He won four junior-varsity races last year," the coach says.

"Good. He's a senior. We'll honor your commitments for this season. But I can't make any promises for next year," Ed says. He stands up and extends a hand. Coach Morris gets up and reluctantly shakes it.

"We just got new uniforms," Coach says.

"You can use them for track."

"We can't. They say 'Cross Country' on the front."

"Take care, Ken," Edward says, dismissing him politely.

Coach Morris leaves the office and stares up at the sky. The season ahead of him just got a lot tougher.

After school, Eric is in the locker room getting ready for football tryouts. Beef and Crush are also there and looming nearby, taunting him. Eric cinches up his shoulder pads and notices that the pads are too big for him.

"Sure you're in the right place, little man?" Beef asks. "Those pads your size?"

"Pee-wee football is down the street at the grade school," Crush says.

"We'll see you on the field," Beef says, pounding his fist into his other hand.

Coach Rick Martinez, a thirtysomething, heavyset man, saunters into the locker room talking with Russell Burke, a senior, the starting quarterback for Regal High. Crush and Beef see the coach and quickly leave. Eric notices them leave and grabs his well-worn football cleats from his locker. He sits down and takes off his tennis shoes. He tries to slide his right foot into the football shoe. It doesn't fit. He tries to force it in. His foot hurts and the toes are squeezed together. His heel won't fit into the shoe. He folds down the back of the heel, steps on it, and puts on the left shoe the same way. He's in a panic. His feet grew but he didn't. Coach Martinez and Russell are at the end of the aisle talking.

"I want you to just go through the motions, light throwing. Just work the arm out. Don't hurt yourself," Coach Martinez says to Russell. Russell notices Eric staring down at his feet. The coach looks over to see what has Russell's attention. Eric can feel the eyes on him as he tries to tie the shoes tighter so they'll stay on. He's the last one left in the locker room.

"Hey, kid, get out on the field. We don't have all day!" Coach Martinez yells.

"Okay, Coach," Eric says. He looks back down at his ill-fitting shoes. He opens up his locker and pulls his tennis shoes back out.

Rushing out to the football field, which is still wet from the morning's watering, Eric is the only kid wearing tennis shoes. He slows to a walk on the wet grass, worrying about how his flat shoes will perform. He sees the offensive players crouching low to the ground, taking their positions. He notices that the spot for wide receiver is open—a position he's very familiar with. He checks to make sure the drawstrings are tied securely at the waist of his gray sweatpants. Walking past the other freshmen and sophomores getting ready to scrimmage, Eric makes a small observation: they all seem much taller than he is. The gap in size is larger. It dawns on him: he's considerably shorter. He resembles his dad, who is also short. He thinks about it and decides, *Oh, well, it didn't keep Dad from playing football. Maybe next year I'll grow.*

Eric joins the formation as a wide receiver at a watery spot on the grass. Looking down, he has the horrible thought that he'll slip and slide in the tennis shoes. Beef and Crush watch Eric, looking smug and delighted.

"I'm gonna have some fun. Kick back and watch this," Beef says across the scrimmage line to Crush before running over to the cornerback position opposite Eric.

"Take a break," Beef mutters to the cornerback, pointing him toward the sideline. Eric gets into position and looks down to find a waterless place in the grass to set his tennis shoes. When he looks up through his face mask, Beef is facing him across the scrimmage line. Before he has time to react, the whistle blows. Beef rushes forward, his massive body hitting Eric hard and dislodging his shoulder pads. The impact knocks Eric to the wet ground. The whistle blows again.

Determined not to look stunned, Eric quickly stands up. He retightens his loose-fitting helmet and shifts his pads back into position. He wipes himself off just in time to see Beef nod in approval to Crush, who stands watching. Coach Morris walks up near the field.

Paul Tate runs up to Coach Morris. "Hey, Coach," Paul says, "You're looking for good runners, right? I know someone."

"You do?" Coach asks.

"Yeah, and he's out on the field."

"Which boy is he?"

Paul looks over and sees Eric, "There he is. Playing receiver," Paul says, pointing to the smallest boy on the field. "He's shaking off the pain."

When the whistle blows again, Eric hesitates, pushing off carefully from the wet grass. Beef hits Eric just as hard, throwing him to the ground like a rag doll. From a distance, Russell looks over with concern.

"That boy there?" Coach Morris asks, pointing at Eric, who is on the ground, shaken up.

"Uh… yeah."

"Nahh. I don't think so. I'll see you at practice," Coach says as he walks to the football field.

"Okay, Coach," Paul says, turning to walk away. He can't bear to see Eric get hurt anymore.

Eric gets up slowly. Coach Martinez comes over and offers Eric a hand.

"What's your name, son?"

"Eric Hunt."

"Eric, do you know why the whistle blows?" he asks, pulling him to his feet, and then retying the shoulder pads.

"Sure. To start or end the play."

"Then what are you doing here, when you should be downfield?" Coach Martinez says as he motions downfield before looking over at Beef. "And you, Beef, you're a tackle, that's offense. Why are you on this side of the line?" Crush chuckles nearby.

Beef turns red around the collar. "I don't know, Coach. There was nobody here to babysit him, so I thought I'd try cornerback."

"Knock it off. No extreme hits at practice!"

The coach turns to Eric. "Kid, you haven't been able to get past the scrimmage line. Do you think you can make it downfield at least once?"

"Yeah," Eric replies. "I think so, Coach."

Everyone returns to their positions. Russell watches with interest, impressed with Eric's tenacity. Eric knows he's faster than Beef and is determined to race right past him. He tries to anticipate the signal. When the whistle blows, Eric tries to charge forward at an angle but his shoe slips on the slick grass. He regains traction but the delay allows Beef to grab him. Eric feels Beef's outstretched hands close around his ankle, sending him face-first into the grass. The whistle blows.

"That's it, everybody," the coach calls. "Give me four laps around the track."

Everyone groans as they slowly start for the far side of the field. Beef ambles over to the grinning Crush. The coach looks down at Eric, who's gathering his strength to get back up.

"That means you, too," the coach says as Eric sits up. "Look at me. You're going to need cleats, real football shoes. And if you don't grow, you better bulk up, start eating and lifting. You got that?"

"Yeah," Eric says, nodding.

"Now get going. You owe me four laps," Coach orders as he writes some notes on his clipboard. Russell walks over to Eric and puts out a hand. Eric removes his helmet to clean out some wet grass. He looks up at the quarterback, surprised that he would help him up. Russell pulls Eric to his feet.

"Thanks," Eric mumbles.

"I used to be small when I was a freshman. Bullies picking on me," Russell says.

"Really?" Eric says, looking at him, surprised at how big he is.

"If that guy bothers you again, let me know."

"Thanks," Eric says as he watches Russell jog toward the track. Eric limps a few steps as he walks toward the track to join the other players already beginning to run. Coach Morris walks up to Coach Martinez.

"Hey, Martinez, do you have any runners I can use?" Coach Morris asks, "If I don't get my team in shape this season the athletic department is going to drop us next year," he adds.

"Next they'll be going after football," Martinez says. "These new kids are all wannabes. They all think they can play football. You can scout around."

"What about that kid?" Morris asks, pointing to Eric. Martinez looks at Eric, who puts on his helmet, cinches the chin strap tighter, and begins to run.

"He has some guts, but he's no football player. Too small. I wish I had some kids with his attitude, though, for the tough games," Martinez says. The coaches walk closer to the track and eye the jogging players. Eric is speeding up on the backstretch, and he starts to pass other players. He overtakes two seniors, then Crush and Beef, who try to stay near him but quickly give up. He goes past one player after another, making his way to the front of the group. Standing inside the track near lane one, Coach Martinez writes on his clipboard. He casually glances up as the players jog past. Coach Morris notices someone partially obscured but moving fast out in lane five. Coach Martinez can't see Eric; his view is blocked by the larger players. He does notice Coach Morris reach for the stopwatch hanging around his neck and start the watch, his eyes glued to the track.

"That kid can run," Morris says, keeping his eyes on Eric.

"Which one?"

"The one with the tennis shoes."

"Oh. Him again."

"Any chance I can have that kid?" Morris asks.

"It's up to him."

"Do you mind if I speak to him?

"Go ahead. He's too small for the team. My boys are gonna kill him. I'd hate to see him get bruised every day."

As they come into the homestretch for the third time, Eric passes the last two runners in front of him. He opens up a big lead on the last lap, and as he finishes, he's passing kids who are a lap behind him.

Coach Morris looks at his stopwatch, "Seventy-five seconds for the last lap. That's pace for a five-minute mile," he says. And in his mind he adds, *and that's with a helmet and pads.*

As the football players strip down and head for the shower, Eric sits on the bench in front of his locker. Beef and Crush rush into the aisle and grab him. Eric struggles but Crush pushes him to the floor. Beef drags Eric by the legs out of the aisle and swings him under the showers with all his clothes on.

"C'mon, you need to cool off. How about a cold shower?" Crush says. As Beef holds Eric down, Crush lifts a bucket of ice water from behind a bank of lockers and pours it over Eric's head. He and Beef pick up some loose ice cubes and stuff them into Eric's pants, laughing. They run off, leaving Eric there, soaked and freezing.

Later, Eric walks slowly home.

That evening Eric sits in his room playing a video game on his computer, trying to forget about the tryouts. On the wall are two certificates for participating in Pop Warner football, but no awards. There is a knock on his door. He sets down the game controller as his dad comes in carrying a shoe box. Dale Hunt is a stocky, athletic man of Irish descent. Eric gets his light green eyes from him. Dale was a good college football player but didn't go pro. He always wanted to coach football when he got out of college, but he settled for a job in sales after he got married. Raising a family became his top priority. Maria, Eric's mother, follows Dale into the room. She is second-generation Mexican-American, medium height and athletically trim. Eric has the same thick black hair and olive skin that she has. Maria works part-time as a nurse in the morning, making time to be home when her son comes home from school.

"How did your first day go?" Dale asks, taking a seat on the bed.

"Not so great. I got picked on again."

"That wouldn't happen if you listened to me," Dale says.

"Dad, look at me, I haven't grown since last season. I haven't gotten any taller over the summer. Now they call me all kinds of names and bully me."

His dad stands and crosses his arms. "If you want kids to stop picking on you, join the football team."

"I did, and it's the football team that's picking on me."

"You'll toughen up," Dale says with his trademark squint.

"Dale, aren't you being a little hard on him?" Maria says.

"All freshmen go through it," Dale says before handing him the box. Eric opens it to find football cleats.

"I noticed your cleats were worn out, so I bought you a new pair to start high school with."

Eric closes the box looks at the side. He reads the shoe size and frowns.

"What's wrong? You don't like them?" Dale asks.

"They're too small," Eric says.

"You just said you didn't grow over the summer. I got your size from the old cleats."

His mom shakes her head. "Honey, I told you they were too small for him."

"Well… I'm not any taller, but my feet grew," Eric says.

"That's a start. Start eating more. You'll bulk up."

Maria intervenes. "He'll grow naturally," she says

"I don't know about that," Eric says as he tries in vain to fit a foot into one of the shoes.

"I was small, too," Dale says softly. "But football changed all that." Eric doesn't want to say what he's really feeling. He doesn't want to disappoint his dad. But he wonders sometimes who he's really doing this for. Does he really want to play football, or is this just his dad's dream? Dale continues, "A few months in the weight room bulked me up." He proudly pumps his arms. "I got respect. Maybe that's what you should be doing instead of playing these computer games."

"These computer games improve my eye-hand coordination," Eric replies.

"So does boxing, Eric," Dale says before disappearing out the door.

Maria reaches for the shoe box. "Can I see those?" she says kindly.

"Mom," Eric ventures. "Have you ever heard of cross country?"

"Of course, honey. I ran cross country in high school."

"Really?"

"Sure did. It wasn't popular back then the way it is now, though. We didn't have fancy outfits or training equipment."

"You're kidding," Eric says. "You were a runner?"

"I even won a couple of races," Maria replies with a smile. "I have many great memories of the team."

"Why didn't you ever tell me about this?"

His mom moves to the door with the shoe box. "Follow me," she says.

Maria takes Eric to the china cabinet that sits in a corner of the living room. On the top shelf, she carefully moves aside the assorted figurines and a stopwatch that had been there ever since Eric could remember. She'd even let him use the watch a couple of times. What he'd never noticed before were the two running medals beyond the watch cord. She pulls the medals out and hands them to him. He looks at the biggest one first.

"State champion?" he asks. "Cross country? Wow, Mom!"

The next morning at school, Eric is one of the many students wandering the hallways looking for classes. Standing at a door, he checks his schedule. It's the right classroom but the wrong floor. Eric walks down the hall toward the stairwell. He looks up the stairs before going up. He sees Beef and Crush standing and talking to each other. Eric immediately turns around and almost collides with a girl coming up behind him.

"Oops! I'm sorry. Excuse me," he says to the very pretty blond cheerleader he's almost hit.

"That's okay," she says, smiling as they part ways. Eric hurries down the hall. Beef and Crush hear the commotion, but when they look, Eric isn't visible, so they resume talking.

Eric walks toward the opposite stairwell. In the hallway, Coach Morris sees Eric and races to catch up to him.

"Hey, wait a minute. I saw you at football practice," Coach Morris says as Eric turns around, surprised.

"I'm Coach Morris, the cross country coach. I saw you run. Eric, is it?" he asks.

"Yes," says Eric as the bell rings. They both acknowledge the bell.

"Have you ever thought about cross country?" Coach asks.

"No."

"You should."

"No, thanks. I'm already going out for football."

"You can change your mind. Coach Martinez will understand," the coach says.

"I'm going to be late," Eric says, trying to leave but the coach steps in front of him.

"I saw you run. I think you have potential," Coach Morris says seriously. He steps aside.

Eric hesitates, then politely excuses himself. "Oh. Uh, okay, but I should be going."

"Going out for cross country is pretty simple. Just show up for practice at the back of the school, outside the locker rooms," Coach Morris says as Eric walks away.

Eric walks slowly toward his classroom, thinking. He would never have guessed that a coach would want him on the cross country team, or any other team. It was the last thing he thought would come of the horrible football tryouts. *I think you have potential.* Eric feels a brief rush of pride. Nobody has ever said he had potential for anything before.

School's out and students are going home. Eric is at his locker putting away his books. He carefully slides the books beside his new football cleats. He looks at the shoes and thinks about his dad as Paul rushes up.

"Hey. We're practically neighbors. I'm three lockers away," Paul says, pointing toward his locker before noticing the shoes inside Eric's. "New cleats? You're not going back to football practice, are you? You should be running."

"After two years of Pop Warner, my dad expects me to go out for the team. He got me the shoes. They're too small, though. I don't know why I even brought them," Eric says, taking the shoes out to show Paul. Beef and Crush walk up and look into the locker.

"New shoes, huh?" Beef remarks.

"I woulda thought you'd get new padded shorts to soften the falls," Crush says.

"Maybe he wants to get up quicker," Beef says.

"We'll see you out on the field," Crush adds, elbowing Beef. They share a laugh as they amble away. Paul turns to Eric.

"Suit yourself, be with those jerks. You know, it didn't exactly look like you were *excelling* at football," Paul says.

Eric gives some thought to the remark. "Nope, I wasn't," Eric says, placing the shoes carefully back inside the locker before closing the door. "I'm gonna try out for running."

"All *right*," Paul says as they walk away.

They pass Beef and Crush standing in front of the locker room.

"Hey, where's your new football shoes?" Crush asks.

"Yeah," adds Beef. Paul and Eric both turn around but keep moving.

"Don't need them. I'm on the cross country team," Eric says. He and Paul turn back and go into the locker room.

Walking out of the room, Eric feels hopeful. The cross country team is gathered on the asphalt area, everyone dressed in the same thick cotton shirts and shorts. Immediately Eric notices separate groups forming. Older boys—probably the varsity team—gather on the right, girls on the left. Somewhere in between, Eric joins Paul near a pimply-faced kid—probably a sophomore—who's eating a candy bar.

Nearby, Crush and Beef exit the locker room dressed in football gear. They wave at Eric to get his attention, and then Beef points straight at him while Crush makes a gesture like twisting something in half with both hands.

"Quitter!" Beef yells, then laughs and turns away with Crush to walk out toward the football field.

Paul turns away. "Those guys won't stop."

"Guys like that never do. Hey, you look pretty serious about running," Eric says.

"I *am* serious. I told you, I'm famous. I have an image to protect."

Paul notices Eric's shoes. "You're not running in those, are you?"

"Yeah, why?"

"You need running shoes," he says, showing Eric his new green shoes with yellow trim. "Like these."

"I can't run in these?"

"You can, but they're not good for distance running. Those are good for short bursts of speed and lateral moves. The midsoles won't last through the constant pounding of long training runs.

This is a specialized sport. Shoes are important. You should check out the Runners Sole store on Fremont Street. They have all the good shoes there."

"I'll check it out," Eric says.

"Oh, great!" Paul remarks with concern, nudging Eric.

"What?" Eric asks, following Paul's gaze.

"See that guy there, with the mustache? That's Barry."

"Yeah," Eric says, looking at a boy with a full mustache and thick brown hair that he spikes up. He looks like he's in college.

"He's a varsity runner. He's in stealth mode—watch your groin," Paul warns.

"Why?" Eric asked.

"You'll see," Paul says, motioning for Eric to keep watching Barry. Just then Barry walks up to the kid eating a candy bar, says "Hey, Rick," and punches him in the groin. Rick doubles over in pain and drops his candy bar.

"Ouch," Rick cries out. "Knock it off, Barry. That's not funny, jerk. I'm gonna start wearing a metal cup."

Eric winces. "Oh," he says. Then he glances quizzically at Paul. "How'd you know he was going to do that?"

"I went to some of their races last year. I checked these guys out."

Barry is pleased with his first attack of the year. "Back for another season of pain? Who's next?" he asks, scanning his potential victims. Barry eyes Eric and Paul, who quickly move out of his reach. Barry chuckles as he walks up to them.

"Hey, you two munchkins. You coming out for cross country?" Barry asks. Eric and Paul stop in their tracks. Paul turns to Barry, unafraid but guarded.

"We're new. I'm Paul, this is Eric."

"What's with the new gear?" Barry asks. "Those clothes need a little grime and sweat."

Rick comes over, "Hey, you guys want any candy? I sell it to raise money for the team," he says, opening up a bag of candy to show Eric and Paul. "A dollar each."

Barry cuts in. "When he's not sellin' it, he's eatin' it."

Barry turns toward the other team members. Rick notices and turns to them as well.

"Hey, guys. Take a look at the new munchkins we've got," Barry says. Mike, a junior, walks over up to Paul and Eric and checks them out. Paul notices Mike's red T-shirt with **<17** printed where a chest pocket would be. Paul bravely speaks up.

"What does that mean, on your shirt?" Paul asks.

"Don't you know your math? This means less than seventeen. This shirt is a highly coveted achievement. I earned it by running a cross country course in under seventeen minutes for three miles," Mike says. "It's not something you can buy, like that fancy outfit. You gotta earn it. Think you can do that?"

"I don't know," Paul says, nudging Eric. "Maybe my friend can."

Eric pokes Paul in the side to shut him up. Mike laughs.

"Yeah, right—with those shoes on you wouldn't make it around the tennis courts," Mike says. "Keep dreamin'—but in the meantime, move away. Don't contaminate the varsity." Mike makes a shooing gesture and walks toward the varsity team. Eric and Paul move a safe distance away but still within earshot and observe the older boys. Mike walks up to the team leader, Vance Davis, a senior. Vance is lean and tan, with a square-shouldered frame and dark blond hair. He's wearing a T-shirt ornamented with the outline of the state of California and the words "State Track & Field Championships" inside the outline. His leg muscles are well defined from all the miles he's run. The GPS watch on his wrist has measured every one of them. Eric and Paul stare at him curiously. Eric nudges Paul.

"Who's that guy?" Eric says softly.

"That's Vance, the fastest guy on the team. He got third in the state track meet in the thirty-two hundred," Paul whispers.

"What's the thirty-two hundred?" Eric mutters.

"It's the metric equivalent of two miles."

"Wow," Eric says in a hushed tone. "Who's that, next to Vance?"

"That's Kyle—he's one of the league's best soccer players," Paul whispers. Mike, meanwhile, looks at all the team members, seemingly disappointed.

"I sense déjà vu. Nothing has changed. We didn't win a meet last year," Mike says, frustrated, to Vance. Vance looks around.

"At least we have five guys this year," says Vance. "If we have a full team, at least we have a chance to win some meets."

"First off, how about we win one?" Kyle remarks. He's a senior, a Latino with a dark tan made even darker by hours in the sun playing soccer.

"You know, Vance lost a sixteen-hundred to an eighth-grader at an all-comers meet during the summer," says Mike. "I believe his name was Bryce. Yeah, that's his name, Todd Bryce."

"Really?" Barry asks Mike.

Vance looks sternly over at Mike.

"Just kidding," Mike replies. "I mean, he would have if the race was a full mile. This Bryce kid was closing fast, just ran out of real estate."

Vance nods. "Yeah, so fast he ran four-twenty-three and I cruised a four-nineteen. He's good, led the first lap and stayed with me for three laps. But he couldn't handle my eased-up sixty-four on the last lap. Lucky you weren't in the race."

"Sub-four-thirty in eighth grade?" Rick asks. "That would be fast for a freshman. Not like the tools we have here."

Eric whispers to Paul. "What's sixteen-hundred?"

"Sixteen hundred meters—the equivalent of a mile," Paul whispers back.

Mike glances over at Eric and Paul. "You notice the two delusional freshmen. Just look at them. Pathetic."

"Whattaya mean?" asks Taylor, another senior in the bunch, who has long brown hair held back with a headband. "That fancy-dressed one looks like one serious dude, ready to race," he wisecracks, gesturing toward Paul.

"He likes to dress up," Mike replies. "He's going trick-or-treating as a runner."

"Check out the other guy," says Vance. "He isn't even wearing running shoes."

"Court shoes," Barry says with disgust.

The sound of the double doors opening attracts the attention of the boys' team. They all turn their heads. As if in slow motion, two beautiful girls step out. One has long black hair and light brown eyes and is wearing a cheerleader uniform. The other is dressed to run. She has medium-length blond hair and light brown eyes, and is about five-foot-six and very fit.

Eric eyes her and nudges Paul.

"Who is that?" Eric asks. He recognizes the blond girl from nearly running into her in the stairwell. *Wow,* he thinks, *she's on the team.* Paul frowns at Eric. "The one on the right is Ellie, and the other one is my sister Vanetta. They're both cheerleaders. Vanetta won't run because she doesn't like to sweat. Can you believe that?" Paul says.

Eric mumbles, "Ellie, huh?"

Mike raises his hand to his forehead to shield the sun and get a better look. "Whoa, that's Ellie the head cheerleader."

"Looks like she's ready to run," Vance says.

"Cross country just got popular," Mike says.

"Ooh, yeah!" agrees Kyle.

Vanetta looks around at all the runners. She whispers to Ellie, "Are you sure you want to run with all these bony half-naked dorks?

"Yeah, I made up my mind," Ellie says with determination.

"Those guys are eyeing us like a pack of wolves. Watch out for my little brother Paul, he tends to trip over his feet. You might accidently run over him. He's the short one over there in his spiffy new running attire." She leans in to whisper, "Freshman!"

Ellie says seriously, "They don't bother me."

"I don't see how you can let yourself get all sweaty."

"I'm okay with that."

Suddenly, a door opens and another cheerleader sticks her head out.

"Vanetta! There you are. Come on, we have practice."

"Good luck running with those creeps—*gross*!" Vanetta says. Undeterred, Ellie turns toward the runners and walks forward, her blond hair blowing in the wind, to join the team, much to the delight of the gawking boys. Vanetta watches for a moment and then disappears inside. Grace, a senior runner with reddish-blond hair, walks up to Ellie.

"Hi. The girls usually hang over on the side, away from the boys. I'm Grace," she says.

"Ellie," she responds, glad to have company. Eric watches the girls from the side, trying not to be too obvious. The other boys are less subtle with their stares.

"This is Katy. She's the fast one," Grace says. Katy is African-American, a sophomore. She's tall and very athletically built.

"I remember you from cheerleading tryouts last year, Katy says. "I didn't make it, so I went out for cross country. I've been doing it ever since. I watched your routine, you're pretty good, very serious."

Ellie smiles, "I try to be. That's why I'm here, to keep in shape. You can try out for cheerleading next season. There's going to be some openings," she says.

Katy shrugs. "No, I really like running. It's my calling. There's nothing like running long-distance. Nothing but you and the road ahead. And it's a great feeling to cross the finish line."

"It's a rush, nothing like it," Grace adds.

The varsity boys continue to shoot glances at them once in a while, but the girls ignore them.

Coach Morris strides out from the locker room and the boys quiet down.

"Good afternoon, everyone. Welcome to Regal High cross country. You'll be learning a lot here—think of it as Cross Country One-Oh-One. For those who don't already know me, I'm Coach Ken Morris, but just call me Coach. I also teach PE here. I'm glad to see everyone back from last year. Welcome back, Harriers. I'm happy to say our roster has expanded. I'm sure we'll have a better season this year."

"Not too hard to be better than dead last," Mike replies under his breath.

Coach Morris eyes each runner as he walks around the team.

"Running is an individual sport," he begins. "It takes a lot of discipline to work hard every day at developing your body to push it to the limit. Running builds character. It's not like any other sport. If you get tired or want a break, you can't pass off to a teammate. You can't sit out for part of the run. There are no substitutes. You have to step up to the line, and when the gun fires, it's you against everyone else. You're racing the course and competing every step of the way to get to the finish line first." The coach takes the stopwatch from around his neck and holds it out. "You're also racing against time. That's your biggest enemy. The untiring finger of the clock! But time isn't only your enemy; it can be your friend. You pace yourself with it, you respect it, you use it to your advantage. You challenge it!" Coach glances around at the runners. "Any questions? Anybody want to back out?" He looks over at Eric. "Anybody want to join the football team?" Everybody looks at Eric. He feels the weight of their stares. He shrugs his shoulders uncomfortably and shakes his head no.

"Let me introduce the two freshmen," Coach Morris continues. "Everybody, this is Paul and Eric. Paul seems to be better prepared. We need to talk about proper attire, Eric."

"Eric must be lost," Mike says. He stares in Eric's direction. "Hey, dude, the tennis courts are over there." The rest of the varsity team laughs, except Rick, who stares absently over at the tennis courts.

"I don't get it," mumbles Rick. The boys grow quiet again before Coach Morris asks for everyone's attention.

"We have another new member," he says, coming to stand beside the cheerleader. "This is Ellie. She's giving running a try. She wants to improve her fitness."

"I'll help her improve," one of the boys comes out with, accompanied by a few hoots and hollers.

"Okay, settle down now," says Coach Morris. "Remember, running can help you improve a lot of things. School, your home life, and your conditioning if you do other sports. Are you all warmed up and ready to go?" He claps his hands. "Okay, varsity, let's see who worked out over the summer; if you're warmed up, I want you to run out to Decoto Road and come right back." He raises his watch again and clicks it. "Okay, go!"

The varsity team takes off, except for Kyle.

"Something wrong, Kyle?" Coach Morris asks. "You waiting for me to say please?"

"Coach, it's the first day. I didn't run over the summer. Don't you think I should run with the girls?"

"Nice try," Coach Morris replies, not amused. "Get going."

Once Kyle leaves, the coach turns to Eric and Paul.

"You're going out the same route, but not as far. From here, go through the park, and when you reach Lafayette, come on back. Simple out-and-back. Got it? I'll see you back here when you finish."

Eric and Paul start off at a steady pace behind the varsity guys. Behind them, the girls start running, too. A few minutes into the run, Eric stops to retie his shoe.

"Go on ahead," he tells Paul. "I'll catch up."

Paul continues. Soon the girls begin to run by Eric.

"Bunions?" Ellie asks, stopping beside him.

"No—blisters," Eric replies as she runs by, laughing.

It's late in the afternoon when Eric and Maria arrive at the Runners Sole Store. The front walls of the small specialty shoe store are adorned with race numbers and running photos. Eric looks past the racks of colorful singlets and shorts as his mom stares at all the selections. Eric notices the shoes, each on its own little shelf, covering the wall near the back and moves toward them. Mesmerized by all the selections, he walks forward to get a closer look. He's dwarfed by the display of shoes, some he can't even reach.

"I've never seen so many running shoes. They never had this much in my day," Maria remarks.

Eric tries to look over all the shoes and sees one he recognizes as the new model Paul wears, but in different colors.

"How are you going to decide on shoes?" Maria asks.

"This one," Eric says, smiling as he looks closely at the shoe and then inside the heel. A sticker inside has the price on it. "But they're kind of expensive."

"I took back the football shoes." Maria smiles and Eric smiles back. A tall, lean salesman walks up with a foot-measuring device.

"Good choice. Place your stocking foot on this and I'll get you a pair," he says, setting it down. Eric steps onto the device.

"Looks like you're an eight," the salesman says.

Moments later, Eric excitedly stands up with the shoes on and begins to run in place as Maria proudly looks on. Eric could not be happier. They are lightweight, the perfect shade of blue, and best of all, they fit.

The next day, in the locker room, Paul is pleased as he looks at Eric putting on the same model shoes he has.

"Nice footgear. I almost got blue," Paul says. Eric proudly laces his new shoes up. Paul slips his shoe off.

"It hugs the foot, good heel cushioning, it absorbs hard impacts, and it's not too heavy. Where did you get the idea to buy those?" asks Paul while holding up his used dirty shoe.

"From you, of course."

"I know. I got good taste."

Eric stands admiring his shoes. The varsity boys run past and notice Eric's shoes. Mike pauses before heading out.

"It's not about fancy shoes or outfits, ya know," Mike calls out. "It's really just left foot, right foot, repeat with speed. But that might be too complicated for you." His voice trails off as he heads out.

"Ignore them," Paul says.

"How can I? They're on me all the time."

The team runs to Maywood Park, where Vance takes the lead, followed by the rest of the varsity boys, who are passing the girls' team, with Eric and Paul not too far behind.

Mike motions to Rick to slow down while feigning foot trouble so the others wouldn't question why they stopped.

"What is it?" Rick asks.

Mike puts on a show, grabbing at his toes as if he's in pain just as Eric and Paul catch up.

"I got blisters," Mike whines. "I'm going to need new fancy shoes," he says in a mocking baby voice.

"This sounds serious. I better take a look," adds Rick with a smirk. "Oh man! That blister is as big as one of Kyle's pimples!"

Eric and Paul run cautiously past them, trying to pay no attention. Mike watches as Eric and Paul disappear in the distance. He turns and grins at Rick, who smiles back. Mike and Rick congratulate each other with high-fives before bouncing up and running toward the community center. They go around the old brick building to the entranceway and disappear inside.

"You think they saw us?" Rick whispers.

"Nah. C'mon, I'll rack. Double or nothing," Mike says.

As Eric and Paul run through the park, Eric begins to move ahead, feeling confident in his new lightweight shoes. He sees Ellie and the girls running together up ahead. He looks over at Paul.

Eric nudges Paul. "Should we pass them?"

"Yeah, we should pass the girls."

They pick up the pace, catch up to the girls, and move wide to pass. Eric slows down next to Ellie to show off his new shoes. He glances over at her while Paul continues on ahead.

"No more blisters," Eric says with a smile.

Ellie smiles sweetly. "I can see that. Nice kicks."

Eric picks up the speed and moves away, catching up to Paul. They continue to put distance on the girls. Eric sees the varsity team up ahead. He makes up his mind to catch up to them. He concentrates on them and speeds up. Paul starts lagging behind.

"Eric, pace yourself," Paul calls out, dropping farther back. Eric doesn't listen and keeps pushing. The varsity team, far ahead, disappear around a corner and out of the park. Eric keeps up his faster pace, but as he nears the corner he realizes that he's working really hard. He turns the corner and sees the older boys getting farther away down the road. Suddenly Eric feels so tired that he isn't sure he can keep running. His pace slows dramatically and he trudges on.

The next day at school, Eric maneuvers his way stiffly through the hallway with Paul. He stops at the locker.

"Man, I'm sore," Eric says. "I wasn't this sore yesterday."

"That's because you tried to catch the varsity," Paul replies. "Remember what Coach said—you gotta pace yourself."

"Aren't you sore?" Eric asks.

"No way. I ran six days a week over the summer," Paul says proudly.

"Every week?" Eric asks.

"Yeah. I usually do my long run on Sunday," Paul adds. "What did you do over the summer?"

"I played computer games and surfed the web." Eric rubs his leg. "There's no way I can run today."

"Don't let the guys hear you say that. Besides, you'll be fine once you get going. Today's just an easy distance run."

"If you say so," Eric says, thinking, *if it hurts this much to walk, how am I going to run?*

"Ignore the pain," Paul tells him. "It's crucial to just keep running—weekends, too. The first two weeks are the worst. You'll feel like a zombie."

"Great," Eric replies.

"Your legs get so tired, they go numb," Paul continues, thrilling over the agonies of his chosen sport. "Then you don't feel anything. Not even tired. It's weird, but that's what happens."

Eric's face is devoid of humor as they walk toward the locker room. "It's going to be a fun two weeks."

That evening, while playing video games, Eric doesn't think much more about what Paul was saying until he tries to get up to go to the bathroom. His legs hurt to move. He shuffles into the bathroom and decides to take a bath and soak his sore legs. He undresses gingerly and carefully steps into the tub. Then, he sprinkles in some sea salt and mixes it into the water. He's just starting to relax when there's a knock at the door.

"Ahhh," Eric sighs.

"Everything okay?" Dale asks from behind the door.

"Yes."

"How's football?"

"I'm in the bathtub soaking my sore muscles."

"Oh," Dale says. "That's normal. You'll get over it in a couple of days… go ahead and use some of my sea salt. Soaking in it loosens up the muscles."

Eric sighs with a bit of relief because he didn't ask if he could use his dad's salt.

Eric doesn't think much about Paul's advice to run on weekends until the next Saturday, when he rides along with his mom and dad to the shopping mall. While daydreaming and staring out the window, he's surprised to see Vance running on the side of the road. He's even more surprised when they pass him again, running the other way, on their drive home. As they fly past him, Eric swivels his head.

"Mom, what time is it?" he asks from the backseat.

"Ten after five."

"Really? Ten after five?" he questions as he fixates on Vance.

"Yes," Maria replies. "Since when are you so concerned with the time?"

Eric doesn't hear her. He's too busy doing the math. They had left for the mall before four o'clock, which means Vance has been running for at least an hour and ten minutes. And he's not done. Vance is running nearly half a marathon, maybe more, out on the road while Eric had been in the video game section of an electronics store. Maybe Paul was right. He just needed to keep at it. Maybe after a few weeks of running, he could run that far, too.

The bell rings and the first class of the morning empties students out into the halls. Eric notices Crush and Beef moving strategically behind him, carrying football helmets, no doubt in the midst of an intricate plan to get him in some way. He's so engrossed in trying to figure out what they're up to that he barely notices Ellie and her friend Vanetta approaching.

"Hi, Eric," Ellie says.

"Oh, hi."

"Are you going to practice today?" Ellie asks.

"Oh yeah, I'll be there." Even though he's still sore, he won't miss the chance to run with Ellie.

Eric looks over his shoulder again just in time to catch Crush's and Beef's stunned faces. As they turn to look at each other, Eric darts away safely.

"That freshman just talked to the head cheerleader!" Crush says to Beef and adds, "Maybe he couldn't find his next classroom and was asking her for directions."

Beef takes his helmet and hits Crush with it. "Get going, you jerk."

After history class, Eric goes to the locker room, replaying the scene in his mind for the hundredth time. As happy as it made him to think Crush and Beef were jealous, he knows once he exits the locker room he'll be in for it. On the asphalt area, Crush and Beef stand waiting for him, but he isn't about to walk into an ambush. He starts to run, hoping that they don't follow him onto the field. Glancing back, he sees that the bullies are not deterred so easily. Beef and Crush are close but not within reach, and they're falling behind. Eric picks up the pace and widens the gap on them. Beef, who's carrying his helmet, flings it at Eric's feet. The helmet bangs into Eric's foot. Pain stabs through his ankle as he falls hard next to the rolling helmet.

"I got to hand it to you," Beef says, coming to a stop beside him. "You're fast for a freshman. But not fast enough."

"You think because you quit the football team you're gonna get away from your initiation?" Crush asks.

In the distance Coach Morris appears and stares in their direction. Beef notices Coach approaching and alerts Crush.

"This isn't over," Beef warns in a whisper.

"Hey, Coach," Crush yells to Morris. "He tripped showing us some running moves." Beef and Crush scuttle away.

Coach Morris hurries over to where Eric sits holding his ankle. "What happened?" He glances over at Beef and Crush. "Did those boys do this?"

"No. I tripped on their helmet," Eric says, too embarrassed to admit he got knocked over.

"If they did this, you better tell me," he demands.

"No, it was my fault," Eric says, looking down at the grass.

"Well, if you want to change your story, let me know," Coach says, suspecting that Eric is covering up.

"I was just clumsy."

"Let's get you to the nurse," Coach says. "Think you can make it inside?"

"I think so," Eric says. He stands and hobbles beside the coach back to the school, burning with anger.

Coach Morris watches as the nurse carefully places a bag of ice on Eric's ankle and gets him to hold the ice against the swelling knot.

"It's a mild sprain. Just enough to get you out of practice," the nurse declares.

"Not the best way to start the week," Coach adds.

"You think I'll be able to run on Thursday? I don't want to miss the first meet," Eric says.

Coach Morris looks at the nurse, "We'll know after you get it X-rayed."

"Stay off your foot as much as you can," the nurse says. "No running for a few days. I'll bandage it up before you go home. We'll see how you're feeling tomorrow." Eric breathes out heavily, frustrated.

Eric limps home from school, wondering what he's going to tell his dad. Maria looks out from the kitchen window and sees

Eric, worn out and limping up the walkway with his foot taped. She meets him at the front door.

"What happened to you?" she asks.

"I tripped," Eric answers. He knows that if he tells her the whole truth, she'll be very upset. Eric hears his father drive up.

"Don't tell Dad. Please," Eric whispers.

"Why?" she asks.

"I don't want to disappoint him," Eric says.

"You haven't told him you quit the football team yet?"

"Not yet."

"When are you going to tell him?"

"I don't know. I'll break it to him slowly," Eric says trying to hurry onward as the door opens. Eric is limping away as his dad walks in.

"Eric. What happened?" Dale asks.

"I tripped on a football helmet," Eric says.

"You gotta watch yourself out there. It's all part of the game. Go soak your ankle in ice water." he says. Eric acknowledges the advice and limps to the bathroom.

"I'll get you some ice," Maria says. She turns to Dale. "I'll take him to get an X-ray."

"Does he need one?" Dale asks.

In the bathroom, Eric sits on the rim of the bathtub and begins to cry in frustration. Maria knocks on the door. Eric fights back the tears and wipes his face.

"Are you decent? Here's your ice," she says behind the door.

"Yeah, c'mon in," Eric says. She comes in and is about to hand him the ice but she looks at his face and stops.

"Are you crying?" she asks.

"No. I just threw water on my face," Eric says.

"Wow, it's really swollen," she says, looking at it and carefully placing the ice on the ankle. "It looks like it really hurts." They both remain silent for a moment. His mom finally breaks the silence.

"Eric, if you want to quit running, I'll understand. Is there anything you want to tell me?" She asks. Eric looks away.

"No," he says, looking down.

"Are other kids bullying you?"

Eric doesn't answer. He grabs the ice. "No."

His mom yields and stands up to go. "If you want to talk, let me know." She stops at the door and turns. "You're going to have to face your father soon and tell him you're not playing football."

Eric looks up. "I know," Eric says. His mom looks concerned.

"Let me know if you need anything," she says before she closes the door.

Eric moves the ice over his ankle. "Ouch!"

"Uniforms?" Paul asks.

"That's right, Einstein. They'll be here in five minutes," Taylor replies. "See this? It's a varsity letterman jacket. It means freshmen get to the back of the line."

Barry is at the front of the line with the other seniors. As Paul walks by, Barry tries to drive the point home by attempting to hit him in the groin, but Paul blocks the blow with his wrist and Barry hits Paul's watch instead.

"Oww!" Barry cries, gripping his knuckles. "You lousy freshman."

Mike fakes a punch at Paul as he turns away and speedily passes the varsity members on his way to the back of the line.

"You know who you almost hit?" Kyle says to Barry, who's looking his hand over for injuries.

"Yeah. One of the new freshmen, who's lucky I didn't kick his ass for jabbin' me with his watch."

"That's Vanetta's little brother," Kyle says.

"Vanetta the cheerleader? No way. That?" Mike asks.

"You serious?" Barry says. "Friggin' genetics."

"What about the other freshman?" Mike asks. "He got any hot sisters we should know about?"

"Nope. He's fair game. He lost the genetic lottery."

At the end of the line, Paul meets up with Eric.

"You see what they tried to do to me?" Paul asks.

"Yeah. What's up with that?" Eric says.

"Just because they got a varsity jacket they think they're kings. Luckily, I blocked his punch but he hit my new watch. It's supposedly shock-proof. I hope it's okay." He squints at the watch. Coach Morris calls for everyone to quiet down.

"Good afternoon, team. For the race on Thursday we'll meet in front of the school at three-fifteen. We'll be going against two schools, a double dual meet. Now, you'll need uniforms for the race. Everybody gets outfitted. Okay, varsity first."

"Guess we wait," Eric says.

They watch the varsity team file through the doors.

"What's a double dual?" Eric asks in a hushed tone to Paul.

"A race with three teams but the scores are totaled separated between only two teams at a time. We'll compete against Rockford for one dual meet and against Hammond in the other, simultaneously. One race," Paul says proudly showing off his knowledge.

"Oh, that makes sense," Eric says.

"Hey, I hear the new uniforms are made of some new sophisticated material, like from NASA," Paul tells him.

"Really?"

"Running has gone high-tech, dude," Paul says.

After a few minutes, the older boys return with their new varsity uniform singlets and sweats. Mike shows off his white jersey as he walks past Paul and Eric, who watch him warily.

"That's what *I'm* talkin' about," Paul says once Mike is out of earshot. "That's going to be us!"

Eric imagines wearing his new uniform, running through the finish line in record-breaking time, arms stretched upward, the tape snapping perfectly as he slows his powerful stride. Ellie and Vanetta would rush to congratulate him. He'd play it cool and swear he wasn't anything special, but they would gush with pride over his talent and beg him to coach them. After he agreed, they would plant kisses on his cheeks.

A jersey hits Eric in the face and he comes back to reality. Coach Morris stares at him.

"Eric, are you listening? Try this on."

Embarrassed, Eric unfolds a thick cotton twenty-five-year-old jersey, once white but now a faded gray, and puts it on. The hole for the head is a little big, and the rest hangs loosely over his chest. An embroidered patch on the front displays an attacking eagle, the wings outstretched upward, head down with spread talons about to catch prey. Just below the eagle are two cloth ribbons, red and blue. It is a decent mascot, Eric decides, compared to what some of the other schools have. It's amazing what counts for a mascot these days.

"Perfect," says Coach Morris, and he tosses the white brushed-cotton shorts and the old-style sweats at him as well.

"You'll grow into it by the end of the season. It'll give you a confidence boost. How's the foot?"

Eric looks down at his bandaged ankle. "Nothing's broken—it feels okay. I'm sure it'll be ready for practice tomorrow," he says.

Eric is sitting on his bed. He places a pillow down where his foot will be. He carefully places the ice pack on his ankle, then delicately wraps the pack around the foot. He slowly turns on the bed and sets his foot on the pillow. With his foot elevated, Eric lies down. He looks at the stopwatch that his mom lent him and clicked the top button, starting the timer.

"Twenty minutes," he sighs. He's convinced that he'll be running soon because he's doing everything he can to be ready. Once settled in and comfortable, he picks up the video game controller that he set beside himself and begins to play.

But despite lots of ice and sitting with his foot propped up most of the evening, he still limps the next day. As he comes out of the locker room Beef and Crush seize the opportunity to harass him.

"What's the matter, Eric? Why you walkin' all funny?" Beef asks, smirking, lumbering toward him in his football gear.

Eric doesn't answer. In the distance he sees Coach Martinez coming toward them.

"Beef! Crush!" the coach yells. "You know why you're jay-vee? Because you're screwing around when you should be on the field!"

"Yes, Coach," they answer in unison.

Beef looks at Eric. "See you in your grave."

Coach Martinez walks over to Eric.

"What happened to you?" he asks, looking at his foot.

"Sprained my ankle."

"Rough sport, that cross country."

"Hey, Coach," Martinez calls to an approaching Morris. "I didn't give you my prize recruit so you could injure him. If I wanted that I would have had him back for football practice."

"Maybe if you kept your boys in line, my runners wouldn't get unusual injuries. He fell over one of your boys' helmets," replies Morris.

"Well, any of my boys give your runners a hard time, let me know."

"You bet."

Coach Martinez returns to the waiting football players as Eric limps over to Coach Morris.

"Eric, you're not thinking of running today are you?"

"Well, yeah," Eric replies. "My foot feels better." He watches as the cross country girls run across the field.

"But you're still limping badly."

"I'm only being cautious. I can run on it. Look, I'll show you." Eric starts to walk, pretending it doesn't hurt.

Coach Morris puts a hand on Eric's shoulder. "I don't know. You might be able to run today, but let's save it for tomorrow." The coach leaves, and Eric watches Ellie, who's running out of the field and off campus.

Peninsula Course

The cross country team assembles in front of the school near the entranceway after the final classes let out. The students leaving school glance at the large digital ground sign to read the announcements. The headline reads:

FOOTBALL SATURDAY

at Wayland

WELCOME DANCE FRIDAY NIGHT

Some of the departing students show enthusiasm after reading the sign. It doesn't go unnoticed by the varsity runners.

"Why isn't our race up there?" Rick asks.

"Ahh, the ignorance of youth. Don't you know by now? It's all about football and basketball," Kyle says.

"And dances," Mike says.

"Running isn't on the school radar," Paul whispers to Eric.

"I never knew it existed," Eric says. Mike overhears them.

"The only running I used to do was from the cops," Mike remarks.

Eric and Paul look at each other. The coach drives up in a team van and opens the doors.

"Okay, team. Let's go," Coach says. The team is full of energy and excitement as they get into the van. The girls get in first, followed by some of the varsity members. Paul and Eric wait patiently. When everyone else is in, Paul excitedly gets in ahead of Eric. Eric notices Ellie near the front in the second row; the first seat is for the coach. Eric thinks about sitting next to her to strike up a conversation but decides there's no chance. Ellie is too busy chatting with the other girls and doesn't even notice him pausing to find a seat. He turns to sit with the coach in front of Ellie, but he's interrupted by Paul's voice.

"Eric, sit next to me," Paul commands. "I saved you a seat." Paul motions for Eric to sit in the middle. He reluctantly walks past Ellie toward Paul. Mike shifts seats, moving in front of Eric to take the seat next to Paul.

"Your reservations are in the back," Mike says, looking at Paul and pointing. "This is for varsity so we can stretch our legs."

Paul gets up and goes to the back, and Eric follows. They take seats, glad to be going to the meet. The other boys pile in, and the van starts up. Paul turns to Eric.

"This Peninsula course is the hilliest and toughest course around. Nobody likes to run it because there's no way to get a fast time, it's so hilly. I looked it up online," Paul says.

"Really?" Eric says.

"Yeah, our school lost two meets there last year. It was also a double dual meet. I looked that up as well," Paul adds. Eric looks up ahead to find Ellie, but his view is blocked by all the tall boys in front of him.

"Oh," Eric sighs, disappointed. He thinks about Ellie through the drive, and then even his concentration on her is forgotten as they approach the Peninsula course.

The course is laid out through a small park nestled between coastal hills, an hour's drive from the school. The first cross country meet of the year is against Hammond and Rockford. The van passes a Hammond school bus parked on the street and then turns into a small paved parking lot. Eric looks out the window at a makeshift sign that reads PLEASE DO NOT PARK ON THE DIRT —CROSS COUNTRY RACES IN PROGRESS. He's excited to see a crowd of bustling people getting ready for the race. This sport is so different. He tried out for basketball in middle school, but he wasn't tall enough. Running seems so natural, something that can let him prove himself. He still wonders how he's going to tell his dad about quitting football. But now he has to focus on the race.

They park near the Rockford team van. As the Royal team members climb out of their van, they see that the grounds are full of parents, fans, and competitors from Rockford and Hammond. They sport team colors and shout cheers. Regal is dressed in team sweats except for Kyle, who wears an old hooded sweatshirt with his team sweatpants. Eric stands on the sidelines, taking it all in. Paul stands next to him watching all the activity. Eric watches runners jog, warming up for their races. He looks past the competitors peppering the trails at a massive hill on one side of the park. He's a little intimidated as he looks up at the hill. Paul turns to Eric and notices his concern. Mike notices Eric as well and elbows Taylor, getting the other varsity boys' attention.

"I've never run a hill before, and that thing looks big," Eric confides to Paul.

"Check out the kid, he's terrified," Rick says. "Don't worry—there's a downhill over there." He points to the other side of the park.

"That is, if you make it that far." Taylor says, laughing along with the varsity guys. They walk into the park and set down their gear. Paul and Eric lag behind.

"Don't worry about them," Paul says, looking over his sweats. "I don't feel as fast in these as I do in my own sweats," Paul says, "but I guess I can get used to them. How about you?"

"They're okay," Eric says with a shrug, more worried about the course than his sweats.

"We should jog the course. You know, scope it out," Paul suggests.

"Good idea."

Coach Morris yells after them. "Hey, where you two going?"

"Going to jog the course," Paul replies.

Coach Morris checks the time. "Paul, you can jog. Eric, stay off your foot. Do some stretching at our camp, and just do a little warm-up right before the race."

Paul takes off for a quick look at the course while Eric starts stretching. When Paul returns, they begin a warm-up routine together with some wind sprints.

"This course is really hilly," Paul says. "How's the foot?"

"Some pain, but don't tell Coach," Eric confides. "You were right—my legs aren't tired today. But I'm really nervous."

Coach Morris returns with a box of pins and stickers for the race. Eric and Paul walk over to him.

"Eric, I don't think you should run today," Coach says.

"What!? Why?" exclaims Eric. The coach looks ahead.

"I checked out the course. It looks too risky. Too many rocks and narrow gullies left from the rain on some of the hills. No good for an injured ankle."

"But Coach, it feels fine. I'll be careful," declares Eric. He looks up at the coach, his eyes pleading.

Coach Morris looks seriously at Eric. "Okay. But if you twist that ankle again you'll be out for a month, not just a few days," he says. "Understand?" He points a finger at Eric.

"Yes, Coach," Eric says in earnest. The coach shakes his head and scribbles their names and school on two stickers.

"Here, pin these on. Anywhere on the front of the singlet." He hands them each a small sticker and a pin. "The course is well marked and Rockford will have people out there to direct you so you don't get lost. Let's head toward the starting line over there," Coach says, pointing to the other thirty-three freshman and sophomore runners who are lining up for the start of the first race.

Time seems to speed up. Before Eric has a chance to notice his nervousness, the starter fires the gun and they're off. Eric immediately sprints to the front, opening a five-yard gap that quickly becomes ten as he breaks away from the field. He's running like a madman, and out of the corner of his eye he notices he's alone. He glances back to see that he has at least fifty meters on the next runner and smiles broadly. His legs are fresh; his feet are light, like they have wings. His lead grows to sixty meters, and he doesn't want to lose it. He feels great. He runs even harder in a bold attempt to run away with the race. But after a half-mile, he begins to get winded and loses speed as well as his smile. His wild start has tired him and he begins to fade. The uneven ground

causes occasional pain in his foot, but the fatigue is far worse. Eric balls his fists and strains to keep going, his breathing labored. The tops of his thighs begin to feel heavier with every stride. His thin biceps start to feel heavy as well. He fights to hold his lead, but it is diminishing. Just before the one-mile mark, he is engulfed by a pack of runners. Eric is now struggling badly. The competitors race around him on both sides. By two miles, he's near the back of the field. Paul catches him.

"C'mon, Eric," Paul says as he strains to hang on behind a couple of Rockford runners. Eric tries to stay with them, but soon he has to let Paul go.

Eric is having trouble even jogging, then shuffling. Even though the pain in his foot is gone, he feels stuck in slow motion. He doesn't know if he should walk, take a rest, give up, or keep going. He decides to keep going.

The other runners are taking a sharp left on the hilly course ahead. Cheers erupt for the main group starting up the hill as they near the spectators lining this crucial part of the course. Eric watches as the fans dash away from the trail to another point on the course to follow the race after the lead runners crest the hill. There's no one at the top of the hill by the time he gets there and only one other runner—Hank, an overweight freshman—is still behind him. Eric struggles up the ridge and totters down the other side. Along the side of the course, Mike, Barry, and Taylor warm up for the varsity race.

"Hey, dude, it may be frosh-soph, but it's still a race, not a jog," Mike yells at Eric. Eric looks at him, utterly exhausted.

Eric thinks, *stopping isn't an option.* Although unable to speed up, he's determined to keep going.

He hears more cheers in the distance and knows the runners are crossing the finish line. By the time he makes it out of the woods and onto the home stretch, everyone has left the finish area except a finish-chute girl, who pulls the name-label off his singlet and sticks it in place number 34 on her clipboard sheet. The last place on the board is 35, reserved for Hank, who is still on the course.

Dejected and weak, his throat burning, Eric wobbles through to the end of the chute, where he meets up with Paul.

"You okay?" Paul asks.

"I thought it would never end. I quit. I'm not going to go through this again," Eric says.

Hank puffs his way past the finish line, comes to a stop, and leans forward with his hands on his knees, catching his breath.

"You don't mean that," Paul replies. "At least you didn't get last. I don't think any amount of explaining could wipe out the negative power of that word."

"That doesn't make me feel any better—I was *next to last*. You ever get last?" Eric asks.

"Yeah. Twice. But one of the times I passed a guy with a half mile to go. I finished, turned around, and saw him run off the course and drop out, which made me last. If I was bigger, I would have gone over and punched the guy out."

"Well, I'm quitting while I'm still next-to-last. I can barely walk."

Hank walks up and passes them, his face flushed bright red.

"Hey, good run," Paul says to him.

"Thanks." Hank grabs the front of his sweaty singlet. "You know what size this is? It's a large. A year ago I used to be a double-X."

As Hank walks away, Paul turns back to Eric. "Wow. He took placing last a lot better than I did. How's the foot?"

"That's the only thing that doesn't hurt."

Hobbling, Eric manages to follow Paul back to the team's camp. Coach Morris stops his conversation with one of the parents and joins his team.

"Nice race, Paul, Eric, go warm down."

"Coach, I can barely move."

"Your legs need it, at least fifteen minutes. We'll talk later."

When Coach Morris leaves, Paul glares at Eric. "Why didn't you tell him you quit?"

"I can't tell him now."

"Why not?"

"The meet's not even over yet."

"Are you sure you're not changing your mind?" replies Paul. "You'll never hear the end of it from the varsity."

Eric and Paul jog over by the parking lot when they hear spectators screaming for the girls' race.

"The girls are near the halfway point," Eric says.

"Yeah, so?'

"Let's go see them run," Eric says. He wants to see Ellie. He forgets momentarily about any pain and coming in next-to-last.

"Why d'you wanna watch a bunch of girls run, anyway?" Paul asks. "I'll be with the guys. I'm going to watch Vance and the rest of the varsity warm up."

"Okay, I'll catch you later," Eric says, watching the leading girls approaching. He walks to the edge of the course. The race is three-quarters done but Eric is determined to cheer Ellie on. He can see Katy, the fastest Regal runner, just behind the leaders. He sees Grace in the middle of the main pack, but he can't find Ellie. He keeps looking and finally sees her in a pack at the back of the field.

"Come on, Ellie!" Eric cries out as she runs past him. The trail narrows up ahead at a turn. Eric sees Ellie get pushed and shoved as the other girls squeeze in ahead of her. Eric is concerned for her as she manages to stay on her feet. She loses momentum and struggles to keep up with the other girls. As she disappears down the trail, Eric runs toward the finish area. As he jogs, he's accompanied by other spectators running to see the finish. While watching the girls cross the line one by one, Eric wonders how well Ellie is going to do. Soon, his question is answered. Ellie has fallen behind and comes in next-to-last, just like him. *Maybe I could talk to her now—we have something in common*, he thinks. He runs around to the finish line and meets her. Ellie is worn out. Eric walks up to her to give moral support.

"Good run," Eric says.

"Those were some tough hills!" she exclaims.

"I know. You did pretty well, though—at least you didn't come in last."

She looks at him. Eric walks next to her. "We both got next-to-last," he says with a laugh. "We have something in common."

"The difference is, you took off too fast. You didn't pace yourself. I didn't have that problem," Ellie says.

"Oh," Eric says. "Yeah, I started out pretty fast, and I just wanted to keep that pace. I guess I was too eager."

Ellie looks over at him. "Look, the last thing I want to hear right now is a freshman telling me that coming in next-to-last is something we have in common. I gotta go warm down," Ellie says.

She goes off to join the other girls, leaving Eric alone and discouraged. *Nice work*, he thinks as he watches her walk away. *I just told her that we're both losers*. Eric turns away to see the varsity team lining up at the start. Eric sees Paul and walks over to join him on the sidelines.

Rick, Vance, Taylor, Mike, and Kyle line up next to the other runners on other teams. Vance looks confidently at the course ahead and takes a few deep breaths. He wants to make up for last season. The gun fires, and the competitors charge across the starting line.

"Go, Regal!" Paul and Eric yell as the runners come flying by. Eric watches intently as Vance cruises up to the front with the leaders. Paul has a pair of binoculars that he looks through.

"C'mon, let's go watch them up the hill," Paul says, jogging off across a field.

Eric and Paul stand on the sidelines near the crest of the hill, watching as the varsity runners climb the hillside just before the woods. Paul looks through the binoculars. The hill shows the strength and weakness of the Regal team. Vance is up front with the leaders, and no other Regal jersey is in sight until the middle of the pack.

"You see where Vance is? He lets the others go ahead of him and gauge how fast they're going. He studies them for a while and when they show weakness, he just passes them," Paul says. Eric borrows the binoculars and looks through them to watch Vance. Two Hammond runners are in the lead, but Vance surges ahead as they reach the top of the hill.

"Let's start walking to the finish," Paul says. They leave with a few other spectators before Taylor, Barry, and Mike begin to struggle up the hill. Going up, Mike and Taylor lag behind the others. Barry drops back even farther, really going slow up the hill. All three Regal runners allow themselves to get passed by competitors on the climb.

Near the finish, Paul and Eric await the finishers.

"Vance is really good," Paul tells Eric. "He's one of the top runners in the state. Look, here he comes."

They watch as Vance exits the woods with a significant lead. The small crowd cheers for him as he sprints to the finish.

"Wow," Eric says. "Look at him sprint. And after running all those hills. How'd he do last year?"

"He was doing well until he got injured after winning league. That cut his season short. He would've made it to state. He did make it in track, though."

A little while later, the Regal team members are all sitting together, putting on sweats and getting ready to go home. Eric sits off to the side of the group with Paul and listens to the guys intently.

"I hate this course. It sucks," Barry complains. "I never run well here."

"You should have run during the summer," Taylor says. "Like Vance did."

Barry sneers at him. "Kiss my you-know-what!"

"Hey, at least you beat Rick," Taylor replies.

"That putz. He quit."

"Hey," Rick jumps in. "I didn't quit. I went out too fast so my legs gave out."

"That didn't stop Eric," Ellie says. "He went out too fast, but he hung in there and finished."

Eric is amazed. After that brush-off earlier, she's just stood up for him. He figures maybe she isn't mad at him after all.

"She knows his *name*. Uhghh!" Mike groans.

"I saw that," says Kyle. "He's got guts."

"He got second to last!" Rick says.

"At least he finished," Ellie replies. "Eric's not a quitter. He stayed tough and put one foot in front of the other."

Paul leans in and whispers to Eric. "Wow, that's coming from a junior. You got a rep. It's too bad you won't be around to enjoy it."

"You know, you shouldn't be spreading silly rumors like that," Eric replies. "Did you see what I did? Man, I felt great at the start. After a quarter-mile, I was winning."

"Yeah, what the heck were you thinking? I looked up and you were way ahead."

"I was too nervous."

Coach Morris walks up and interrupts Eric's account of the race.

"Eric, I need to speak with you," Coach says. Eric gets up as the whole team eyes him. Coach puts his arm around Eric's shoulder and pulls him aside to talk privately.

"This is good," Coach says as he stops, "You surprised me. Sprint out and die in epic fashion. I don't want to see that again."

"I don't know what got into me, Coach, but I felt great when I started," Eric says. He decides not to mention the feeling of wings on his feet. The coach is looking straight into his eyes. Eric is nervous.

"Eric, do you want to stay on the team?" Coach asks. Eric is afraid to answer. Did the coach hear him say that he wanted to quit? Did Paul say something?

"I'm not sure," Eric mumbles. The coach holds the eye contact, keeping him on the spot. "Coach, I did terrible out there. I can't believe I came in second to last. I thought about quitting, but now I'm not sure."

"Look, this isn't about coming in next-to-last, or dead last for that matter," Coach Morris says. "It's about strategy and running smart. It's not a football field where you charge off as fast

as you can. It's a cross country course, and it's three miles long.
You have to learn to pace yourself. You made a beginner's
mistake. I saw your first half-mile. That's not winning. This is an
endurance sport; what counts is what place you're in at the end.
You can learn tactics. That means staying *near* the front and using
your speed at the end. If you're going to learn pace, you need to
get a watch. It's an essential part of your equipment, as important
as shoes. Understand?" Coach says, pointing his finger right at
Eric.

"I understand."

"Your last mile should be the same speed as your first
mile—or faster. If you run a seven-minute first mile, the last mile
should be seven minutes or less. That's called a negative split.
Your watch will tell you that. You follow me?" Coach says.

"Sure," Eric replies and looks at him. "I never knew about
that."

"I recruited you because I see potential, but you have to
believe in yourself. Are you in or out?"

"I'm in," Eric says emphatically. After a moment, he says,
"What if I went out like that and just kept going?" His teammates,
almost in unison, turn from Eric to look at Coach Morris.

The morning sunshine peeps through Eric's window. He's already
up and dressed in his running clothes, sitting on the edge of the bed
with his mom's stopwatch from the cabinet, which she has let him
use. He winds the necklace-like lanyard around his wrist. He
starts, stops, and clears the watch. He'll ask his mom for a digital
wristwatch at some point, but he likes the way the thin red hand on
this old-style watch clicks along, then snaps straight up when he

resets it to zero. He thinks he has it figured out. He remembers the coach's words: Pace yourself. Go faster at the end—a negative split. Satisfied that the watch is secured around his wrist, he walks out of the room. It's still very early in the morning, so he tiptoes through the house, making sure he doesn't wake anyone up. The sun is now over the horizon.

The early sunlight warms Eric as he stands in front of the house. He takes a deep breath, holds out the stopwatch and clicks it on. His legs are stiff as begins his run on the street. There is little traffic, so he decides to take advantage of the free space on the edge of the street. He's enjoying the freedom of running on the open road and likes the idea that he's not being chased by those two bullies. He's even confident about going into the park. Those goons won't be up this early. He can enjoy the scenery and the smell of grass and trees. His legs slowly loosen up and his stride lengthens. He's starting to feel good—he doesn't even feel any pain in his ankle anymore. He has to be careful for the rest of the season. He can't be getting hurt anymore. The park is quiet and the sun is behind the trees; the air is still cool. He strides through the park, unaware of the ticking watch in his hand. He knows a mile will be up when he gets to the school. He's measured it on the internet: it's exactly one mile from his house through the park and to the corner of Regal High School. As he arrives at the edge of campus, he holds out the watch and clicks the button on top. He slows to a stop in a few steps and looks at the watch.

Six minutes and twenty-five seconds, he says to himself. He clears the watch, turns around, and clicks the button again. *Okay, under 6:25*. He heads back the other way and picks up the pace. He takes the exact same route as before, even trying to remember his exact path for accurate timing. As he winds through the park, the air is warmer and the morning sun peers through the trees. Eric is focusing on the run, enjoying the challenge of trying for a faster second half, when he sees Beef and Crush walking straight toward him. Eric knew that this was a risk, but he's not going to let these guys ruin his run. Time is of the essence. The two boys are surprised to see him approaching.

"Hey, *freshman!* What are you doing in our park?" Beef yells as they spread across the path, arms out, ready to tackle him as if they're on a football field. Eric keeps running so he won't mess up his time. As he approaches them, he remembers the slippery grass at football practice. He veers to the right side of the path and the bullies move with him. Beef laughs, thinking of how slow Eric was that day at practice. He widens his stance. Crush moves farther left to intercept Eric, staying on the edge of the path with one foot in the grass. The space between the two punks increases as they get ready to grab Eric as he runs toward them. His confidence grows with each sure-footed stride on the dry path—no water this time. He sprints, planning to run right between them faster than they can anticipate it. He knows he can apply the fake he was unable to use on the drenched grass. He bears right, then cuts back into the middle of the path at the last instant, straight for the gap between Crush and Beef. Crush is caught flatfooted and fights to shift back toward Eric. Beef, also unprepared, is in an awkward stance to generate any real power to his fist. With his clumsy swing toward Eric, he is unable to deliver a solid punch. As Crush dives desperately at him, Eric jumps, thrusting the watch forward to protect it, and makes it through the gap. The airborne Crush scrapes Eric's back and continues full-force into Beef's open arms, knocking the wind out of Beef and throwing him off balance.

The two bullies spin around. Beef shoves Crush toward Eric.

"Get him!" Beef gasps through the pain in his lungs.

The bullies charge awkwardly onto the path, their shoes slipping in the wet grass. Eric glances back to see them losing ground behind him. They have nowhere near his speed now, and he's been running for well over a mile. Soon they come to a stop, panting and grimacing. Beef is making a high wheezing sound. Eric glances back once more, sees that he's out of danger, and relaxes to a comfortable pace. He's pleased with himself for pulling off the football move.

Crush says "Forget it" between gasps, one hundred meters behind him. "We'll get him next time."

"Yeah, at the lockers, where he can't run," Beef says, fighting for breath with his hands on his knees. They glance at each other, trying to look menacing rather than defeated, and start walking slowly.

Eric reaches his starting point at home, tired but not too out-of-breath. *Wow, that was a close one*, he thinks as he comes to a stop. Just in time he remembers to stop the watch. He looks at the time. *Five-twenty! More than a minute faster for the second mile. I should get those guys to hassle me more often.* He walks into the house. His mom looks up and notices the watch in his hand.

"What was your time?" She asks.

"Five-twenty for the last mile," Eric says, showing her the watch.

"That's great," she says. "Let's put this away for now." She takes the watch and carefully unwinds the cord from around Eric's wrist. "I'll get you a better one to train with. A digital wristwatch that you can wear."

"Thanks, Mom," Eric says. In spite of the drama he's just gone through, he feels good about his time and knows he can beat the pace the coach talked about. And he employed strategy. He learned the lesson.

That evening, Eric is eating dinner at the table. His dad enters the kitchen with his hands behind his back and smiles at him proudly.

"I have a surprise for you," he gloats.

"Really?" Eric asks. His dad produces a bag from behind his back. He takes out a shoe box and holds it up.

"I picked up a pair of size eight-and-a-half football shoes."

"That's too big," Eric says.

"I know. I got them larger because you'll grow into them," Dale says.

"But Dad, that's too big," Eric insists.

"Not for long. In the meantime, just wear two pairs of socks. Easy fix."

"Great—one size fits all," Eric mumbles.

"Where's the other pair? I couldn't find them."

"Oh," Maria says quickly. "I took care of it. I took them back"

"You did? You could have told me."

"I'm sorry," Maria says, "but Eric has some good news."

"He does? What is it?" Dale looks at Eric.

Eric sets his fork down beside his half-eaten plate of chicken. "I joined the cross country team," he says.

Dale puts his trademark wince to use. "Are you kidding me? Why would you do something like that?"

"You know I was a cross country runner," Maria says defensively.

"That was different."

"Different how?"

"It's not a real sport. It's just running," he says.

Maria gives him a straight, no-nonsense stare. "Do you realize that cross country is the purest of sports? That you need guts and determination to succeed?"

"It's just...I thought he was going to play football. He's been playing for two years."

"The coach says I have talent," Eric speaks up.

"What coach would put that nonsense in your head?"

"The cross country coach. Coach Morris."

"He had his first race this week," Maria says, her face softening. Eric looks at his mom with curiosity.

"He did? How did you do?"

"Thirty-fourth."

"How many were in the race?" Dale asks sarcastically.

"Thirty-five."

"Talent, huh? I think this Coach Florist isn't running on all cylinders."

"It's Coach Morris, Dad," Eric says.

"Don't worry about it," Maria assures him. "It was his first race. He'll do better next time. Give him a chance," Maria says. Eric looks at his dad and feels confident enough to tell him the truth.

"Dad, I'm not interested in football. I never really was. I don't even like it. It's your sport, and it was great for you, but it's not for me."

His mom is surprised and listens proudly. Dale is silent for a while, then blurts out, "I thought football would be a way for you to be accepted, get respect, and maybe eventually get a scholarship. It worked for me. I really want you to go to college."

Eric can't think of how to answer. His mother steps in.

"Give him a chance to enjoy his first year of high school, let him find himself. Then we'll worry about college, okay?"

Dale gets up from the table, looking like he's been benched during the fourth quarter. He puts the football shoes back into the box.

"I'll take these back in the morning," he says. "Excuse me."

Eric and his mother watch Dale leave the kitchen. Maria hugs Eric, who breaks away to make it a short hug.

"C'mon, Mom, I'm too old for that mushy stuff."

Maria smiles at him. "Can I come to some of your meets to watch you run?"

"Well, sure."

"You sure I won't embarrass you in front of your teammates?" she asks playfully.

"Naw, it's okay. Besides, nobody else has a mom who's a state champ. No hugs in front of the guys, though," he says. She hugs him again and he playfully resists. "C'mon, Mom!" he says, squirming. She surprises him with a kiss on the cheek before letting go.

Griffith Park Invitational

The next week at school Eric is walking through the campus when he sees Beef and Crush. He stops, relieved to see they're occupied. Beef is watching Crush crushing aluminum cans and shooting them like basketballs into a recycling bin. He's a bad shot and misses more than he makes. Eric also sees Rick, holding his ever-present bag of candy, talking with a few underclassmen. He's eating a candy bar, trying to make a sale by demonstrating how tasty it is. Eric makes a beeline to his locker. He's opening it when he hears a faint but familiar voice from far off. He turns: It's Ellie, talking with her other cheerleader friends down the hall. Eric pretends to look for something in his locker, stalling so he can see her without being too conspicuous. He takes his jacket off and puts it in his locker. He takes the jacket out and puts it back on. He looks up again. Ellie's dressed in her cheerleading uniform, like the others. *There must be a practice*, he thinks. Eric looks more closely. He likes the uniform, but he also likes her running outfits. He wants to say hi, but shyness holds him back. He needs a good reason. He tries to think of something he could say to her. Maybe he could relay a message from the coach—but what would it be? He could ask her about the Griffith Park race—no, it has to be something good, so he won't look like a dork like the last time. Suddenly Paul's head pops into Eric's view from a foot away.

"What are you looking at?" Paul inquires, blocking Eric's view with his face. Eric closes his locker and mumbles.

"Nothin'."

Paul turns to glance to where Eric is looking, then turns back.

"You shouldn't be looking at her."

"Why?" Eric asks curiously.

"She's not serious about running."

"So what—she's still pretty cool."

Paul holds firm. "You don't want to hang out with a cheerleader like my dumb sister."

"That's no big deal," Eric says, looking at Paul. Out of the corner of his eye he sees Vanetta meet up with Ellie and other cheerleaders. The girls all walk off together.

"She's in a different league; you don't hang out with cheerleaders. That's what football players do," Paul says.

Eric looks over Paul's shoulder one more time. Ellie and the cheerleaders are gone. The bell rings for class.

"See you at practice," Paul says, hurrying off. Eric pulls his biology book out of his locker.

In biology class, Eric stares out the window, thinking of Ellie. He doesn't care much about what Mr. Lopez, the teacher is writing on the board: *Study for Your Biology Quiz!* History is boring but science is cool. Eric likes watching the chemical reactions of different elements. He's good in math and great on computers. All those years of playing video games may pay off someday. Maybe he'll be a computer engineer. He can't concentrate on any of that right now. His focus is on training for the next race. As he looks out the window he notices some dark clouds up above. He never really thought about the rain much before, but now that he has to run, it has more significance. He sees a few drops fall on the window and then a cloudburst hits the school. The bell rings, and he grabs his biology book and sticks it under his jacket. He cautiously walks into the hallway, on the alert for Beef and Crush, and meets Paul.

"Hey, you getting ready to run?" Paul asks.

Eric gives him an incredulous look. "You're kidding, right? It's pouring."

Paul looks at him and laughs. "What do you mean? Just because it's raining, you think you don't have to run?" he asks.

They look out the front door of the main hallway at the deluge. "We're not going to run in that," Eric says.

"Don't let Coach hear you say that," Paul says. Eric looks at him in disbelief before looking out at the rain again.

"You have to run no matter what the weather is," Paul goes on. "You think the weather's going to stop a meet? You better be at practice or Coach will make you do push-ups. I'll see you there."

The rain has not let up when Eric puts his books into the locker after his last class. He starts jogging across campus but when the large drops pelt his jacket, he sprints in an attempt to stay dry. He doesn't slow down until he reaches the overhang at the locker room entrance. A few of the varsity cross-country boys are at the lockers, talking. They don't hear Eric come in.

"So what's it going to be, Barry?" Mike asks. "You with us?"

"I don't know if I should blow off practice," Barry says warily. "I didn't have a good race. But it's really coming down now."

"That was a hilly course," Taylor tells him. "You're better on the flat."

"Yeah. We better go, Taylor," Mike says. "I don't want to hear him whine again like he did after the race."

"I'll show you who whines," Barry replies as Eric walks in and goes to his locker on the other side.

"Where you off to?" Mike asks Eric.

"Practice. Aren't you guys running?"

"Did you notice the rain, genius? Didn't you hear what the coach said? Practice is cancelled. You want to get pneumonia?"

"No," Eric says, looking skeptical. "But I thought we had to run no matter what."

"We're going to the library. You coming?" Mike asks. "Let's go, guys."

Mike pulls out a notebook, closes his locker, and leaves with Taylor and Barry. In the quiet locker area, Eric listens to the rain pounding the roof. The room is empty. *Maybe Paul was wrong about running in the rain,* he thinks. *These guys have to be right. Paul's a novice. He must be overzealous.*

Smirking, Mike, Taylor, and Barry step out of the gym next to the locker room and watch Eric running away.

"You're a dirty heel, Mike," Taylor says, slapping him on the back.

"What? I just saved his life. How do you know he wasn't going to catch pneumonia?" Mike says, laughing at his own joke. "C'mon, let's go tell Coach Eric's not running."

The next afternoon, the cross country team is gathered behind the school to do a workout. Vance and Grace are conspicuously absent. Taylor notices that Rick is wearing a new singlet with a Velcro strip on the back. A little late, Eric comes out of the locker room.

"Isn't that a triathlon top?" Taylor asks.

"Yep. Now it's a cross-country top."

Eric joins the team gathered for practice on the asphalt area. He's barely on the field before Coach Morris calls him over.

"Where were you yesterday?" Coach asks, his voice stern.

"What do you mean?"

"Practice. Don't tell me the rain scared you off."

Eric is about to defend himself when he glances at Mike, who is standing with Taylor and Barry behind the coach. They're all making ridiculous sad faces in his direction.

"I thought it was cancelled because of the rain," Eric says innocently.

"If you wanna be on this team, you gotta run any time, rain or shine. No excuses," Coach Morris barks. "Give me twenty-five push-ups. After that you can catch up to the team.

Eric nods uncomfortably and walks to a spot on the grass.

"Anyone else want to do push-ups instead of running?" Coach asks, looking around at the group. Silently, they all shake their heads as Eric gets down on the grass and does his push-ups. Paul, watching, can't believe that Eric hadn't shown up the day before. The varsity boys are enjoying watching Eric's push-ups.

Irritated, the coach starts looking around at the others. He turns and walks off, reading his clipboard.

After Eric is done with his last push-up, he gets up and wipes the grass off his hands. Paul goes over to Eric.

"What happened yesterday?"

Eric's arms are tired, but he's more mad than anything else.

"I showed up, but Mike told me that Coach cancelled practice because it was raining."

"And you believed him? You should know by now that those guys are liars," Paul says. Eric nods in agreement.

"You run yesterday?" Eric asks Paul.

"Yeah, I ran. Everyone else got soaked, even the girls, but not me. I was prepared for the elements. I got this really cool rain gear."

Eric laughs. "You have an outfit for everything," he says. "But look what I've got." He shows Paul his new watch. "I got it when Coach said I had to pace myself better."

Paul scrutinizes the watch. "It's okay, but it doesn't have all the functions my watch has," he says.

"It's got a stopwatch function," Eric says defensively.

"Well, I hope so! But mine also has a compass, and a GPS signal to map courses, or to find my way back if I get lost," Paul says.

"Look, the most important thing is to time yourself, so you can compare your workouts, right? That's what Coach says."

Coach Morris's voice interrupts them. "Eric, you done?" he shouts.

"Yes, Coach," Eric says, standing nervously, as if at attention.

"Then get back over here and join the team! What are you waiting for, an invitation? You too, Paul, get over here."

"Yes, Coach," Eric and Paul say in unison. They quickly join the other runners. Eric looks for Ellie among the girls but doesn't see her. He wonders if she ran in the rain yesterday as well. He walks over to Grace.

"Hi, Grace—have you seen Ellie?"

"She's at a cheerleader meeting," Grace says. "Don't worry, she'll be here. She misses you just as much as you miss her." She turns to Katy and they share a laugh. Eric sheepishly turns away. He's flustered, but relieved that Ellie wasn't here to see him get yelled at and made to do push-ups. The coach comes up with his clipboard, taking roll.

"Where's Vance?"

"He's still doing his seven-mile warm-up," Mike says. "Guy's ambitious."

The other varsity boys laugh as Eric and Paul exchange surprised looks.

"Where's Ellie?" Coach demands.

"She's has a pep rally meeting," says Grace. "She's running late."

Just then Ellie emerges from the double doors of the girls' locker area. Eric watches her as she takes her place among the girls. She's back in her running outfit and as beautiful as ever. Eric can't help but smile.

"Just in time before the tardy bell, Ellie," Coach says.

"Sorry, Coach."

Coach lowers his clipboard to his side.

"Okay, everybody, here's the workout. Everybody's doing the same run. Go down Fremont for two miles, turn left on Eighth Street and go another two miles, turn left on Lafayette and come back to the school. That's six miles. I'll be out in the van, so stay on the course. No short cuts," he says, and he takes an extended look at the varsity guys, especially Mike and Barry. "Hear me?"

They all mumble, "Yes, Coach."

"Okay, go!" Coach starts his stopwatch and waves them off. Eric and Paul start their watches as they take off with their teammates. Vance appears from the opposite direction and runs past Coach Morris.

"Sorry I'm late, Coach," Vance says as he runs by. He picks up the pace and catches up to the girls, startling them as he flies past. Eric and Paul turn to check out the commotion and see Vance bearing down on them, his sweat-soaked shirt sticking to his thin muscular frame. He passes them quickly and proceeds to pass the other varsity runners.

As the runners approach the mile-and-a-half mark, they see Coach Morris standing on the side of the road with a clipboard and stopwatch. Vance is far ahead, with Barry, Mike, Taylor, and Rick trailing behind. Eric and Paul are next, ahead of the girls. Katy has moved ahead of Grace and Ellie, who watch as she extends her lead on them.

"You know, Grace? You don't have to stay with me," says Ellie. "I know the course. I don't want to slow you down," Ellie says.

"You're not slowing me down. This is a good pace," Grace says.

"Looking good!" Coach Morris calls out as the runners pass him. "Nice pace, keep it up!" he yells at Eric and Paul as they run by.

Coach Morris shakes his head when he sees Kyle, behind Eric and Paul and only slightly ahead of Katy.

"C'mon, Kyle, what's taking so long?" he asks.

"Had to make a pit stop," Kyle says, embarrassed, as he runs past Coach Morris, who's walking back to his van as Katy passes him.

"You should have thought about that before! Nice work, Katy, keep up the pace. Go get Kyle," Coach says. Katy glances over and nods.

"Good going, Grace, Ellie, keep it up," Coach says. The girls smile as they run by. After the last runners are safely past, Coach Morris starts the van and pulls out. He honks as he passes the runners.

Kyle watches the van drive on ahead. When it disappears, he turns to the approaching girls, smiling as he slows down.

"Hey, ladies. Looking good."

"Get lost, Kyle" the girls say in unison.

As they approach Eighth Street, Eric and Paul are maintaining their distance behind the varsity.

"How do you feel?" Eric asks Paul.

"Not great, just okay," Paul says. "Go ahead and speed up if you want."

"I feel good," Eric says. "I think I will."

"Maybe you can catch Rick," Paul says. "He's starting to drop back a bit."

They make a sharp left on Eighth and Eric pulls away from Paul and closes in on Rick, who hears his footsteps and glances back. He sees Eric approaching and speeds up briefly, but he can't hold it and slows back down. Eric catches up again. Rick tries to get in his way but Eric goes politely around him.

"Excuse me," Eric says as Rick warily acknowledges him. Rick drops farther back behind the freshman.

"I need more energy," Rick says, reaching around behind his back. He opens a Velcro flap on his triathlon-style shirt and pulls out a candy bar. He quickly unwraps and eats it.

Meanwhile, at the back of the group, Kyle is running comfortably between Grace and Ellie.

"Shouldn't you be up with the guys?" Ellie asks.

"Not today," Kyle replies. "You see, I listen to my body. Today it says to go easy and run with the girls."

"He's just running to stay in shape for soccer," Grace says to Ellie.

Kyle smiles at both of them and looks at Ellie. "Maybe you could put in a good word and get the cheerleaders to come to the soccer games." Kyle combs his black, curly hair away from his face with his hand.

"I don't think so," Ellie replies.

"Nice try," Grace says. Grace and Ellie laugh and look at each other. Then they spread out just in time for Kyle to run into a hanging tree branch because he's too distracted by watching the girls.

"Ouch!" Kyle cries out, stopping to compose himself. He looks ahead through his watery eyes and sees the girls laughing as they run away.

Eric comes home early evening with his gym bag over his shoulder. He finds his father in the living room on the couch looking at a photo album.

"Hi, Dad," he says, his voice somber.

Dale catches the tone and looks up. "What's wrong, son?" he asks.

Eric drops the gym bag and sits next to his father.

"I didn't do so well today."

"What happened?"

"The coach yelled at me."

"Yelled? What for?"

"For not running in the rain yesterday. He yelled at me in front of the whole team."

"That's his job"

"And he made me do twenty-five push-ups."

"You know how many times I got yelled at by coaches for screwing up in football? I lost count."

"Really?"

"Yes—when I was starting out. It's part of learning any sport."

Eric tries to see the pictures pasted into the album. "Whatcha looking at?"

"It's my scrapbook from high school."

"Can I see?"

Dale moves the scrapbook toward Eric and points at a picture. "This is me playing football." He points at an article on the same page. "This is when I was a junior. I made the varsity team at running back. They wrote about me fumbling the ball in my first varsity game. We lost the game because of that."

Eric looks enthusiastically at one picture after another.

"Is that you?"

"Yup."

"Wow. You look so young there. Look at those uniforms! They're totally different from what we have now. What's that one?" Eric points.

"That was just after I ran down the field, went out of bounds, and ran right into the coach on the sidelines. We bumped heads. I had a bump on my head for a week."

Eric laughs. "What about the coach? At least you had a helmet on!"

"Yeah, he wasn't too pleased," says Dale, turning the pages to look at more photos and articles. He points at another.

"This is my senior year, when we won the state championship. I never ran so hard in my life. I was pretty fast, like you. They clocked me at ten-six for the hundred-yard dash."

"Really? Wow, two state champions in the family," Eric says proudly. He turns the next page to reveal about ten envelopes.

"Those are letters from coaches who were recruiting me."

"Wow," Eric says, impressed. The two of them continue looking at articles and photos in the book.

"Don't worry about your coach, he'll forget all about it tomorrow," Dale says, putting his arm around Eric. Eric hugs him back. "Now get some sleep."

"Good night, Dad," Eric says, grabbing his gym bag before going into his room. His father resumes looking through the scrapbook, reminiscing.

The next afternoon, Mike, Rick, Taylor, Kyle, and Barry are running a distance workout together. The run takes the guys past assorted storefronts. They take turns looking back to see Eric gaining on them. He's about two blocks behind, but he's determined to catch up to them. He's still mad about yesterday but he's decided to ignore them and outrun them. He draws closer—one block behind, then half a block—and notices the varsity guys duck between parked cars to continue their run on the sidewalk. His view of them is now blocked by cars and the occasional truck and bus. Eric reaches a designated corner and turns. They guys are gone.

Confused, Eric slows almost to a stop. The sidewalk is empty, and there's no one on the street. He looks back to see if he passed them without knowing it. No one's there. He realizes that they must have hidden from him somehow. *"Some teammates,"* he thinks, and keeps running.

When Eric walks into the locker room after his run, he sees Mike, Rick, Taylor, Kyle and Barry on the other side of the room, getting into their street clothes. They haven't seen him. A big group of football players is between Eric and the group. Eric opens his locker but waits next to it, trying to hear what the cross-country guys are saying.

"Do you think we ran far enough?" Rick asks.

"Who cares? We worked up a sweat," Mike says.

"Yeah, after we left the store," Barry says.

"Hah! Did you see that kid Eric out there?" Mike asks.

"What's that saying? The loneliness of the long distance runner?" Taylor says.

"He looked kinda lost" adds Rick.

"Lost his blankie," says Mike.

"Huh?" Rick says as the guys laugh.

"Coach's new friggin' pet. Did you hear Coach say he could try to keep up with us?" Mike says.

"What gall. He can't run with us. Who does that creepy shrimp think he is? He should be playing soccer with the other Mexicans. Right, Kyle?" Barry says.

"Hey, man, are you color-blind? Just because I play soccer doesn't mean I'm Mexican. I'm Puerto Rican, you putz."

"That freshman's the putz. Remember he showed up in those tennis shoes? Where'd he get those, the ninety-nine-cent store?" Taylor asks.

"You know, next time instead of ditching him. I'll run him off the road," Mike promises.

Eric has heard enough. He grabs his clothes out of his locker and bundles them up under his arm. He slams the locker door shut and runs out.

The varsity guys stop and look up in time to see Eric vanish out the door.

"You think he heard us?" Barry asks.

"Oops," Taylor says.

"Big deal. Who cares?" Mike says.

They all break out laughing, giving each other high-fives.

Eric, head down, bumps into the coach on his way out of the building.

"Eric, slow down. Are you okay?" Coach asks.

"I'm late. Gotta go, Coach. See you tomorrow," Eric says, racing away. The coach pauses to watch him rush off, still in his running gear, a bundle of clothing under his arm. Then walks into the locker room.

Eric runs into his house. His mother greets him from the kitchen.

"Hi, Eric—how was practice?"

Eric races right past her and down the hallway.

"I gotta take a shower," he says, running into the bathroom and leaving her speechless.

Hot water runs down his tired body. He starts to cry, and the tears blend in with the running water. He stays in the shower a long time.

Later in his room, Eric lies on his bed in the dark. There is a knock at the door.

"Dinner will be ready when your father gets home," his mom says from the outside.

"I'm not hungry," Eric moans and rolls over and puts a pillow over his head.

"Is everything okay?" she asks. Eric doesn't answer. His mom opens the door and enters the dark room.

"Why's the light off? What's going on?" she asks. She turns on the light and sees Eric lying on the bed with a pillow over his head. "What's wrong, honey?" she asks.

"I don't think I'm gonna run anymore."

"Why?" she asks, taken aback.

"It's not for me," Eric says.

"Why do you say that? Is it something about the team?" she asks.

Eric doesn't answer.

"Is it the coach?"

"No," Eric mumbles.

"Well, who is it?" she presses.

"The guys don't like me because I'm Mexican," Eric says.

His mother sits on the bed and puts a hand on his shoulder.

"You know, when I was your age. I had trouble with some kids at school. I wasn't like everybody else," she says.

Eric turns to look at his mother.

"What do you mean? Because you were Mexican?" Eric looks curiously at her.

"I was the only Hispanic kid in my class. Most of them were white—we had a few African Americans. They didn't accept me. I felt different. The other kids ignored me, wouldn't talk to me. I was an outcast. But eventually, I earned their respect," she says.

Eric looks at her intently. "How?"

"Around Christmas time, my mom and I made wonderful tamales wrapped in corn husks. We had a lot left over, so I took them to school. The teacher asked me to share some of my culture and the tradition of the tamales with the class. They were a big hit. Everybody was asking questions and curious about my background, and actually being friendly for once. Even some kids in the class who'd never spoken to me all semester came up to me. After that, they treated me like everybody else. The point is, you're in a new school, you're an outsider, and they have to get to know you," she says, looking at him.

"The varsity guys hate me," Eric says. "I was catching up to them in practice today and they ditched me. They don't want to run with me. The other day they told me that Coach cancelled practice because of the rain. I got yelled at because they all lied. Today they said I should be on the soccer team because I'm Mexican. So what's the point?"

"What did you do when they ditched you?" she asks.

"Well, I just kept going. I finished the workout"

"You did the right thing. Don't worry about them. They're only hurting themselves. You'll see. But you made a commitment. Just go to practice and do what the coach says. Do the workouts and get better. You know, it could be worse," she says.

"Worse? How's that?"

"Eric, there's something I need to tell you."

"What?" Eric looks at her.

"When you were born, I wanted to name you Lupe, after your grandfather, but your father didn't want me to. He thought the name would make you a target for bullies, especially if you got on the football team. He didn't want his son to go through what he went through when he was in school," she says.

Eric props himself up on the bed. "What did he go through?" he asks.

"Your dad's real last name was McGillicuddy. It's also a word that people use to call something that there's no specific word for—like a whatchamacallit. His dad changed it to Hunt because he was getting bullied so much," she says.

Eric laughs. "McGillicuddy," he says.

"Shh. Don't tell him I told you that story." She gets up and walks to the door. Eric follows.

"Mom, I really like your tamales," he says.

"Good, because that's what's for dinner," she says before they leave his bedroom.

It's early Saturday morning when Eric wakes up. He usually goes back to sleep, but today is different. He gets up and grabs his running shoes.

As he steps out of his house, the neighborhood is quiet and serene. Eric jogs down the street toward El Paseo Road. He reaches the old highway and stops at the city limit sign, which is tall and large, with two posts at each end holding it up. Eric stands under the sign and stretches a bit before taking a deep breath. The sign is the start/finish banner for the run that Eric has planned. He starts his stopwatch and begins to run. Heading out, he notices that he's running into a slight breeze. Eric looks up at the trees above him, their branches blowing. He likes the wind in his face and rushing through his medium-length curly hair. He feels alive. Traffic is always light on the old highway. He comes to an isolated intersection at Verdugo Road and looks at his watch:

20:35. He turns around. Now, with the wind at his back, he runs faster with less effort. There are still very few cars. Eric listens to the rhythmic sound of his shoes hitting the gravel-strewn roadside breaking the silence. He doesn't mind the solitude, the loneliness. He accelerates when he sees the city limits sign and runs under it, stopping his watch. He looks at it: 38:50. *That's 18:15 on the way back*, he thinks. Feeling good about his time, he jogs home, thinking about the course. It's just what he needs to keep track of his progress: a warm-up to El Paseo Road, then just the old highway with minimal traffic. No congested intersections, all the way to Verdugo road. It's simple, just one street. Out and back.

It's Tuesday afternoon and Eric is dressing to run in the quiet locker area. Coach Morris comes in and is surprised to see him.

"Eric, practice isn't for another forty-five minutes."

"I know, Coach," Eric says as he finishes putting on his shoes. "Can I get a few miles in before practice? You know, to warm up."

"Okay, but don't tire yourself out, you're still new at this. Practice is at Crescenta Park today. You have some serious hills to do. They're called The Dips—a few half-mile hills strung together. We'll do all of them a few times, so you don't want to be tired already. Make sure you're back in time to ride with me and the team to the park."

"Then is it okay if I do my warm up to Crescenta Park? I know how to get there."

"Okay, but be careful, don't run hard, and watch the traffic," Coach Morris says. "See you there."

Katy, Ellie, and Grace are in front of the school waiting for Coach to arrive in the van. They're joined by Paul. He's anxious and pacing around. The van turns the corner and stops in front of the cross country team. Paul turns to the girls.

"Have you seen Eric?" He asks.

"I haven't," Ellie says. Katy shakes her head.

"Me neither," Grace adds. Coach Morris gets out of the van and opens up the doors. Suddenly, a beat-up red Camaro pulls up next to the van. Barry is at the wheel, Mike's in the passenger seat, and Taylor's in the back.

"Coach, Eric's not here. I don't know where he is," Paul says.

"He's gone on ahead. He's running to the park," Coach says. Paul and Ellie are surprised.

"I hope he doesn't get lost," Paul says, concerned.

"That's pretty far," Ellie remarks.

"I hope he's got a compass," Mike says with a laugh. The coach turns to address the boys in the Camaro.

"C'mon boys, get into the van," Coach says.

"Is it okay if we drive ourselves?" Barry yells out.

Mike pops his head out. "Yeah, we know how to get there."

The coach hesitates. "You know I'm not too fond of going separately unless you're warming up. We ride as a team."

"Just this once, Coach?" Mike pleads.

"Okay, but drive safe. No stops along the way. I'll see you up there," Coach says.

"If we see Eric on the road we'll make sure he's going in the right direction. Tell Kyle we can't wait," Mike says with a forced smile as the Camaro burns rubber pulling out and driving away.

"Slow down," Coach yells out at Barry. Shaking his head, Coach turns toward the team. "Let's go, get in. We have people waiting for us."

Kyle rushes out from the school to see the Camaro driving away.

"Hey! Wait up!" Kyle yells, coming to a stop in front of the team. "They ditched me."

"Get in, you come with us," Coach says.

Eric makes his way to the main road and jogs down the hill to Gale Street, then takes a left at the gas station. He's passing the grocery store when the sound of a honking horn catches his attention. He turns just in time to see the red Camaro catching up to him with a white butt hanging out the window. Barry is at the wheel, honking madly.

"Hey, freshman. Look at this," Taylor yells out. Eric isn't rattled. He figures it's Mike sticking his butt out the window. He thinks it's a pretty foolish thing to do. Mike and Taylor wait to catch the look on Eric's face while they pass. Then, Taylor pops outside to take a swipe at the bare butt, and Mike scrambles back inside just in time. He tugs up his shorts and Taylor slips back inside. They both twist around to laugh at Eric. Other cars are honking now, some of the drivers laughing at the scene.

To his horror, Eric sees his mom's car approaching directly behind the Camaro. She slows beside him just long enough to yell, "Eric, don't snack. We're having rump roast tonight."

"Okay," Eric says as she continues on. He hasn't told his parents much about the varsity boys. What is there to tell, except that they relentlessly pick on him? There wasn't anything his parents could do about it. He tried to picture his mom showing up at practice and beating the varsity at every race. Laughing, he forgets about the Camaro.

Eric arrives at the park just ahead of the van, more tired than he thought he'd be. The boys are already outside the Camaro and stretching. Eric stops close by. Vance is already there, too. He's the only other runner besides Eric to get to the park on foot. Mike notices Eric stopped at the parking lot, breathing heavily and bent forward to recover. Eric straightens up and sees Mike and the other varsity boys motioning and snickering at him.

"Hey, the Vance wannabe looks totaled," Mike says.

"He'll love The Dips," Barry says.

Eric turns to see the girls getting out of the van, followed by Paul and Kyle. Eric walks over to join them.

Mike motions Taylor and Barry to lean in closer.

Mike whispers, "Here's the plan..."

"Wow, this looks tough," Paul tells Eric as they view the hilly layout. It looks like a rollercoaster: steep uphills, with no flat ground before a long downhill to the next hill.

"They call it The Dips," Eric says. Coach Morris walks up to them.

"Don't let it scare you," he says. "This workout is designed to break up your rhythm and develop your strength. Up, down, nothing the same for long. If you're prepared for anything, you'll always have an edge." He walks over to the team. "Okay, everyone, let's go."

The coach starts his watch, and they all take off. The pecking order is established immediately: Vance lopes to the front, the varsity team follows. Eric and Paul are next, a step back, and the girls trail behind. After the first hill, Vance is all alone out in front. Going up the next hill, Eric is sandwiched among Mike, Taylor, Barry and Kyle. A few meters behind them is Paul, who's just ahead of the girls. Suddenly Mike picks up the pace and races up the hill, getting ahead of Eric and Kyle. Barry and Taylor fall back, jogging easily, saving themselves. Mike reaches the top ahead of Eric and the other boys, but then jogs, allowing Eric and the other boys to catch up. Paul stays ahead of the girls, but coming down the second hill he's falling farther behind Eric and the varsity. Ellie and Grace fall back as well, but Katy manages to stay just behind Paul. Up the following hill, Barry charges ahead of Eric. Kyle has fallen back to join Taylor and Mike as they relax going up. Barry slows down at the crest of the hill and looks back to see how close the others are. They all jog the downhill to recover, but when they reassemble as a pack, Eric finds himself boxed in again. Taylor makes his charge up the next hill. Barry and Mike slow up in front of Eric. Eric has to back off to get around them, and then he strains to catch Taylor, leaving Barry and Mike behind. Kyle has lost all contact with the group. Eric thinks, *Why do these guys keep dropping back and speeding up?* He's working hard to stay with Taylor, but no matter how tired he is, he won't show it. *Maybe running those extra miles before the workout was a bad idea*, he thinks. He should have gotten in the van with the other runners, maybe sat next to Ellie and had a conversation. He keeps running, just trying to stay with the leader of the group, not racing. The last hill is the toughest. He's sandwiched in again, unaware of the plot against him. Barry moves in front of Eric. Mike, the instigator, sprints ahead, straining past Barry, Eric, and Taylor. Eric moves around Taylor and notices him and Barry suddenly slowing down to get behind him while Mike charges up the hill. As Eric chases after Mike, he finally figures it out: They're trying to keep him from winning by taking turns sprinting up the hill. *Nice strategy*, he thinks. There's a lot to learn about running. He laughs to himself. Let them have their fun. After all, he's got tired legs from the long warm-up. He finishes the last hill right behind Mike. They've managed to keep Eric from being the first of the group to get to the top of any of the hills. And they've taught him a valuable lesson.

After the last uphill, the boys relax, relieved. The final downhill brings the varsity together again and they head toward the finish. Barry glances around and sprints, getting a jump on the others. Taylor and Mike take off after Barry, leaving Eric behind. Eric sprints, but it's too late. Barry swings his arm up in triumph as he finishes ahead of Taylor and Mike. Eric doesn't mind coming in behind them. After the finish, they all walk and recover. As Eric walks back along the trail, Kyle runs past and glares at him.

"Don't think you can beat me, freshman," says Kyle. "I'm just taking it easy. I'm staying in shape for soccer."

Eric ignores him. Just then, Paul runs down the trail toward the finish.

"Come on, Paul, looking good," Eric says. Paul, exhausted, just glances at Eric as he runs by. Katy appears, not far behind Paul.

"Good job," Eric says.

"Thanks," Katy says. Eric turns back down the path. Ellie and Grace, the last finishers, run past him.

"C'mon, Grace! Good job, Ellie!" Eric shouts. Eric walks over to Mike and the other varsity boys and smiles. He looks directly at Mike.

"Nice strategy—looks like you won," Eric says, then turns away and goes to join Paul at the van. The varsity boys look at one another, surprised that he figured out their scheme. They shrug and head to the drinking fountain.

Eric sits in the back of the van while the coach drives the team back to school. *If they're calling that a race,* he thinks, *then I beat each varsity boy up more hills by chalking up the best average going uphill—except Vance—beat me. And I didn't need a strategy—I just ran.* He looks out the window and smiles.

Friday, at the local park, the cross country team meets after school for a short practice before the Griffith Park Invitational race the next day, Saturday. The coach gathers the runners together and stands in front and prepares to speak.

"Listen up!" Coach Morris calls out. "Tomorrow for the Griffith Park Invite, we meet at seven. That's seven a.m., people." He looks directly at Mike.

"What?" Mike says.

"After all the hills you have been doing, it should be a cakewalk," Coach says.

"Coach, I'm still sore from the hills on Tuesday," Mike says.

"That's to be expected, you'll be fully recovered tomorrow," Coach says. "Today, you'll do a few wind sprints and a longer warm-down."

"That's usually just the warm-up," Eric whispers to Paul.

"You'll do eight fifty-yard dashes," Coach commands. A few of the varsity boys groan.

"Yeah, and these are shorter," Paul says to Eric.

"This will get your turnover back; get the legs used to running fast again. There's a long downhill tomorrow. Okay, girls go first and the boys' follow," he says.

The girls line up near the coach for the first sprint. The boys mill about behind them, waiting their turn. Eric watches Ellie getting ready to run. He wishes he could talk to her, get to know her better. He watches her lining up and looks down at her shoes. One of her shoelaces is untied as she gets ready to sprint. Should he say something? After all, he doesn't want her to trip over her own shoelaces. The boys might laugh at her like they make fun of him. He walks up to her and taps her shoulder.

"Hey, Ellie, your shoe's untied," he says.

Ellie looks down to see her loose shoelace. "Thanks, Eric," she says, tying her shoe and smiling at him.

Coach Morris calls out. "Are you ready, Ellie?

"I'm ready," she says, double-knotting the shoelace.

"Go!" Coach yells out. The girls take off.

"Gotta go," Ellie says over her shoulder as she sprints away. *She sees how the varsity team treats me,* Eric thinks. *Wow, she must be paying attention to me.*

Paul interrupts his thoughts. "You ready?" Paul asks.

"Yeah, I'm…" Eric says before the coach yells "Go! Stop daydreaming!"

Eric jumps into a sprint to catch up to Paul. They slow to a stop after fifty yards. The girls are taking their time getting together at the starting line.

"Hey, Paul, I have a question," Eric says as Paul resets his watch.

"Yeah?"

"Do you notice how the guys on the varsity treat me?" Eric asks.

"Yeah, I noticed. Everyone notices. They do it because they're jealous of you," Paul says as the coach yells for the girls to run.

"Go!"

"Really?" Eric asks glancing at Ellie as she takes off.

"Of course," Paul claims. "You have more discipline and ability, and you're a freshman. They're afraid you're going to beat them," he says, walking up to the starting line. "At least you've got a good reason."

"Go!"

"They're just plain mean to me," Paul says, leaving Eric in the dust. Paul and Eric stop talking and run the workout to the coach's orders. After the seventh sprint the entire team is collected at the far end of the field. The girls are on the line awaiting the signal to run. All the boys are recovering and take their places behind the girls and wait. Mike nudges Barry in the ribs. Barry turns to him. Mike makes a pool-shooting gesture with his arms.

"We on?" Mike asks.

"Yeah, we're on," Barry says, agreeing and smiling.

Coach Morris yells, "Stampede!" The girls run back toward the coach. Vance is alert and takes off after the girls. Kyle sees Vance and starts sprinting as well.

"That's us," Paul says to Eric. Paul dashes off with Eric slightly behind.

"Mike, Barry, Taylor! Are you listening? Stampede means everybody!" Coach yells out. The three boys start running and finish behind the others.

"Now we'll do a warm-down. Varsity boys, twenty minutes around the park. Everybody else do fifteen. After that you're free to go," Coach Morris says. The kids take off running and the coach heads to the van. Running in the back of the varsity pack, Mike glances around back to make sure the coach isn't watching. He motions to Barry and they dart off course. Eric and Paul notice them slip away into the community center.

On Saturday morning Eric is up early. As he leaves the house he notices the bright sun peeking over the horizon. He starts off down the sidewalk, clutches his gym bag that contains his team gear. He passes the paperboy on the sidewalk. On the way, he notices a boy up ahead coming his way and getting closer. He can't remember his name, but he's sure he's seen him at school. The boy is dressed in party clothes from the night before. His jacket is wrinkled and has a drink stain on the chest. He notices Eric wearing sweats and carrying a gym bag.

"You're on the cross country team, aren't you?" the party boy says. "There's a meet today?"

"Yeah, Griffith Invitational. You're a senior, right?"

"Yeah. Maybe later, I'll come over and cheer you guys on but right now I gotta go home and get some Z's."

"Sure—thanks," Eric says. He starts to say something more, but can't find the right words. "See ya later then," he says instead. *It feels good to be a part of a team*, he decides, *even if the members are competing against each other. People start to notice you.*

At Griffith Park, Eric immediately notices the two large banners marking the start and finish lines. About fifty other teams and some 600 runners have already descended on the field. Every picnic table in sight has been claimed by spectators and still more people are lounging in the grass on blankets and in lawn chairs. Eric looks over to see his mom approaching. She seems lost as she looks around for Eric and the Regal team. He walks over to greet her.

"Mom, we're over here," he says, getting her attention. "Did dad come?"

"He had some work today. Sorry," she says. Eric is disappointed but stays upbeat. They walk back to the team. Paul notices Eric and Maria.

"Hey, Eric, over here," Paul calls out. "This is my dad. Dad, this is my friend Eric."

"Hi," Eric says to Paul and his dad.

"Bill Tate," Paul's dad says to Maria and Eric. Coach Morris comes up to them and smiles.

"Dad, this is Coach Morris," Paul says. Paul's dad extends his hand.

"Hello, Coach. I'm Bill Tate, Paul's dad."

They shake hands.

"Coach Morris, this is my mom," Eric says. "Mom, Coach Morris." The two shake hands.

"Nice to meet you, Mrs. Hunt. You have a fine runner here."

"Thank you, Coach," Maria beams. "I'm glad to see Eric take an interest in cross country."

"Mom was a cross country state champ in high school," Eric says proudly.

His mom waves a hand in the air. "Oh, that was a long time ago, but I still like watching races."

"What was your name then?" Coach Morris asks.

"Back then it was Hernandez."

"Maria Hernandez?"

"That would be me."

"I remember reading about you in the paper. You won quite a few races." He turns to Eric and pretends to whisper. "Boy, you got some shoes to fill. You got a state championship to prepare for. How about you get started by warming up. You too, Paul."

Eric says good-bye to Maria and heads out with Paul for an easy jog.

"Your mom was state champ?" Paul says. "That's so cool!"

"Yeah, and I didn't even know about it," Eric says proudly.

Paul looks at him like he's crazy. "Did I miss something?"

"No," Eric replies. "It's just that I didn't even know what cross country was a few weeks ago. Hey, I gotta find a bathroom."

"Okay, I'll see you back at base camp," Paul says.

Eric looks for a bathroom and immediately regrets not going before he left the house. The line wraps around the building and inches forward slowly. Ten minutes later he hurries over to where Regal High has set up camp. Paul is peeling off his sweats with his dad standing nearby. Coach Morris spots Eric and Paul and walks up to them.

"There you are," Coach Morris says. He hands them numbered bibs.

"Now listen up, I don't want to say this twice. Every course is unique and requires unique strategies. This course starts out hilly, so I want you to start slow. After you turn around and hit the downhill, use the gravity to go fast. Just let go and fly down."

Eric and Paul nod, absorbing every word as they pin the numbers to their singlets.

"Don't be nervous. Have a good race, and I'll see you both at the finish. Now go before they start without you."

Paul hands his sweats to his dad and follows after Eric.

Paul's dad turns to Coach Morris. "Usually I'm invisible, but today I get to hold his sweats." He watches the boys join the others lining up at the start.

The starting area is incredibly quiet in the final seconds before the race. Eric and Paul fidget with their shoes. All along the line, the runners are in motion, doing last-minute stretches and checking to make sure their number bibs are secure. Eric is nervous, looking around and clenching his fists.

"I gotta go to the bathroom," he says.

"Are you kidding? You just came from there didn't you? It's probably just nerves," Paul says.

"Really? It's not my bladder?"

"Once you start, you'll relax and forget all about it. Just run, but don't let thirty-three people finish in front of you."

Eric looks determined as they take their places. Paul holds out his fist. Eric makes a fist and they bump knuckles for good luck. Both stare ahead, intent on the task before them.

The gun fires and the race begins. Maria watches the start anxiously from afar. Paul's dad and the coach are next to her.

Eric and Paul start slow and are swallowed by the crowd of runners moving at a quick pace. A fast runner, in a red uniform with yellow trim, sprints ahead of everyone and establishes a lead before they reach the trail. When they get there, Eric is mid-pack alongside Paul, about forty runners back from the leader. They pass the one-mile mark, and Eric leaves Paul and starts to move up the field.

About six minutes later, Eric is passing spectators, including his mom and Mr. Tate, at a sign that reads 2 MILES. He surveys the scene ahead: he's about forty meters behind a pack of three leaders. As they continue past the marker, the group begins to splinter; one of the competitors slows his pace. A minute later Eric passes the runner and continues to gain on the remaining two.

At a sign reading 800M TO GO, Eric is within ten and twenty-five meters of the two runners. The closer one glances back at him, worry on his face. Eric realizes that he isn't very tired. His energy is up and he isn't nervous anymore. His adrenaline kicks in. He speeds up and quickly passes the next runner. Holding his pace, he soon overtakes the other kid as well. It's an open trail ahead. Eric glances back to see the others falling farther behind. He feels that running is the perfect thing to be doing. *If only Dad could see me now, he'd agree*, he thinks. He's grateful that his mom came to cheer him on.

Coming down the hill, he finishes with a sprint and glances back as he comes to a stop. The next runner to finish is more than a hundred meters back. Flushed with pride, Eric is met by a coed with a clipboard who peels off the label from the front of his bib and sticks it on a page.

Walking out of the finish chute, Eric sees Coach Morris heading his way.

"Great job, Eric," he says, slapping him on the back. "What an improvement! From second-to-last to second place overall! You've come a long way in a short time."

"Second?" Eric asks.

"Nearly last to nearly first. That's a massive jump."

"You mean I came in second?" Eric says, his smile fading.

"Yeah. No one was ahead of you but Bryce, in the red. The Skyline kid."

"I thought I…" He stops himself. He didn't win. And the other kid was so far ahead that Eric hadn't even seen him.

He begins to look around for a kid in a red uniform. As if on cue, a redheaded guy in the Skyline red-and-yellow walks up to Eric and Coach Morris. Eric tries to hide his disappointment as the winner, who's about three inches taller than he is, offers his hand.

"Hey, good run," Bryce says.

"Thanks, you too," Eric replies, still shocked by the news. The winner jogs away to warm down. A couple of other freshmen from the race pass by and congratulate Eric.

"Bryce was able to go out fast and still win. That takes a good fitness base," Coach Morris tells Eric as they walk back up the hill. "You're building yours. With a little guts, sweat, and willpower, you'll start a little faster each time and be closer to the leaders. It's a good goal to use to motivate yourself."

The kid who Eric passed for second place near the end, a thin blond guy with DANA HILLS printed across his blue singlet, walks up to Eric. "Nice move, man," he says. "You smoked me."

Eric shakes the Dana Hills runner's hand, surprised and moved by the camaraderie and respect the other competitors display toward him. He turns back to see more runners sprinting toward the finish. Paul is among them. Thinking over what Coach Morris said, he cheers Paul on as he nears the finish line. Eric's smile returns, fresh with possibility.

Moments later, he turns to find his mom squeezing through the crowd. "Congratulations, Eric! You did great out there." When she reaches him, he gives her a big hug without a second thought.

"Oops," he says, letting go quickly. "I'm a little sweaty."

Paul sees Eric and jogs over. They begin to walk around looking at the other teams.

"How'd you do?" Paul asks catching his breath.

"I got second to some guy from Skyline."

"You came in *second*?"

"Yeah, I didn't know he was ahead of me. I thought I won. I didn't even see him."

"Big deal—I never see the leaders. Second! That's fantastic! Hey, I didn't see you either after about a mile—you took off!"

"I should have pushed myself harder. I'm going to go out faster next time," Eric says, a determined look on his face.

"I'm afraid to go out fast," Paul says. "But if you're serious about it, you need to get some racing shoes, like mine and Vance's. They'll cut seconds off your time."

"Racing shoes? I thought I fixed that problem already."

"You've got good trainers, but they're way too heavy for the speed you're talking about. Racing shoes are a lot lighter, with super-thin soles. You just wear them in races."

Eric is distracted as they pass Todd Bryce, who's talking to his coach. "That's him," he says to Paul.

"Please, no more freshman races," Todd is saying. "Can't I stay in varsity so I can have some competition?"

His coach pats him on the back. "We'll see."

Paul looks at Todd and whispers to Eric, "That's the kid who almost beat Vance in that sixteen-hundred! He's the guy who won? Jeez, Eric, you don't have to feel bad about that!" He looks over at Eric and is surprised to see a determined glare on his face.

"I'm gonna challenge the varsity," Eric tells him.

"Varsity? It might be safer to go after Bryce," Paul replies. "Just be careful," he adds, staring at the Regal varsity boys in the distance.

Late that evening, Eric sits at his desk. He hasn't started his homework, even though he can expect a test any day. He's too busy looking up at his new medal prominently hung on the wall over his desk. The front of the medal shows two runners leaping over a log between trees, but Eric is thinking about what's engraved on the back: SECOND PLACE. He looks at his computer screen, which shows the results of the race on the high school running website.

"Todd Bryce," mouths Eric as he types the name in the search box. He navigates to the search box in the running site and types the words "Bryce" and "Skyline" in the search box, then clicks on the top result. The page opens to a cross country preview. Eric finds Bryce's picture and reads the text.

> **Todd Bryce** is a freshman at Skyline HS. Can the heralded age-group star live up to his advance billing?

The bedroom door is ajar and Maria peeks in.

"Time for bed. School tomorrow," she says.

"Okay," Eric says before turning off the computer. He knows he has to study, but he's too tired. He'll open a book tomorrow when he's more awake.

On his way to class the next day, Eric bumps into Beef coming out of the bathroom. Beef tries to grab Eric but Eric is too fast.

"I'll get you," Beef says, trying to follow Eric, who rushes through the crowded hallway and disappears among the students.

The classroom is already full of students when Eric runs in and slams the door. He hears the room go quiet. Everyone turns around to stare at him.

"Sorry," he says. "A draft caught the door."

"As I was saying," says Mr. Lopez, "the Biology test is on Friday." He glares at Eric. "Make sure you study."

Embarrassed, Eric goes to his seat. Now he has two tests to study for, and he hasn't opened a book. As he sits there, thinking about Todd Bryce and how to beat him, he doesn't pay attention to the teacher or the lesson. Time flies by without Eric even noticing. Suddenly, the school bell rings and the students dash out of their classrooms and into the halls. Eric navigates through the hallway to lunch. Before he enters the cafeteria he spots Ellie walking in the same direction. He pretends to read the lunch menu posted on the wall.

Ellie casually walks up behind him and blurts out, "I'd skip Thursday if I were you," she says, standing beside him. Eric looks at her nervously.

"It's that stuff in aluminum foil, tuna surprise."

Eric smiles at her.

"Congrats on getting second place at Griffith Park," Ellie says.

"Oh, yeah, thanks," Eric replies. He wishes he had won. That would really impress her, but he doesn't say anything. A few students walk by. They look at Eric with Ellie and whisper to one another as they enter the cafeteria.

"You know, I almost joined the football team," he says.

"You seem kinda small for football," she says.

"My dad wanted me to," he confides.

"I can relate—my mom made me join cheerleading."

"Really?"

"Yeah, I didn't like cheerleading at first because I thought the girls were snobbish, but I got to know them, and then I became head cheerleader. Now they respect me. Running's cool too."

"I think running's way better than football. My height doesn't matter. The other runners, they came up to me after that race and congratulated me! That was so cool. And the more I run the faster I get, and the more I like it. It's such a rush."

"You know what? You should run with Vance."

"Yeah, right. Come on, he's a senior."

"So? I'm sure he'd be glad to have you along. Just ask him."

"Okay, I'll think about it."

The bell rings and Ellie checks her watch. "See you at practice."

"Yeah, see ya."

As soon as she's around the corner, a boy rushes up to Eric.

"Hey, man. You know her? What'd she say? Get her number?"

"Not telling," Eric says, walking away.

The cross country teams assemble after school in the grass next to the asphalt area. Eric hooks up with Paul, who's stretching and getting ready to warm up.

"Come on Eric, aren't you going to stretch?" Paul asks. He's wearing a new orange top with a circular design in lavender and orange shorts to match.

"I'm already warmed up. I just did a mile around the track," Eric declares. Vance runs up, and sits on the grass near Mike and Barry, and starts to do some stretching. Eric looks over at him, thinks for a bit, and then stands up. "I'll be back," he tells Paul.

Eric approaches Vance, keenly aware that the other runners are watching him. Beef and Crush come out of the locker room with a football. They notice Eric, and Beef motions for Crush to go out for a pass in Eric's direction. Beef and Crush begin throwing the ball to each other as they get closer to Eric and Vance. Mike nudges Barry to look up. Ellie is talking to Grace and Katy. Ellie sees Eric standing next to Vance and summoning up his courage.

"Hey, um... Vance. Would you mind if I run with you on your warm up?"

Vance continues his stretching and squints up at him. "Sorry. I warm up by myself. No offense, but you'll only slow me down."

Embarrassed, Eric takes a step back. He glances toward Ellie and the other girls. Katy and Grace turn away, pretending not to see. Ellie looks as if she wants to come over, but Katy begins talking to her and she can't break away. Ellie mouths the word "Sorry" to Eric before she shyly turns back to Katy and Grace. Barry and Mike snicker as Eric starts to walk away. Eric notices Crush nearby and then sees Beef throw the football as hard as he can. The ball soars straight toward Vance. Focused on his stretching, Vance doesn't see the football coming right at him. Without thinking, Eric sprints forward and deflects the ball just before it would have hit Vance in the head. Vance looks up just in time to see what happened. Crush chases the football bouncing away on the grass.

"Stop screwing around, you morons," Vance yells at Beef and Crush.

"Sorry, man," Beef calls back. Crush grabs the football. While running back over to Beef, Crush has a big grin on his face that only Beef can see. Vance stops glaring at Beef and Crush and turns toward Eric and nods.

"Thanks, man."

Eric nods back and walks away. Mike and Barry snicker.

"Who does that charity case think he is?" Mike grumbles.

"Trying to kiss Vance's ass," Barry adds.

"That stunt with the football, he probably planned it," Mike says.

"You think? Hmm, yeah, maybe he set the whole thing up," Barry says. They both laugh.

Ellie smiles warmly as she watches from the distance with Grace and Katy. They resume talking amongst themselves. Eric walks up next to Paul, sits down, and begins to stretch.

Paul whispers, "What are you doing talking to Vance? He doesn't care about freshmen."

Eric doesn't respond. He looks at Ellie, who's in conversation with the other girls and looks away, disappointed. Paul interrupts his thoughts.

"Hey, you see the results from the Griffith race?"

"Yeah, I did last night."

"Bryce, your nemesis, was all over the running site. He wasn't just in the results, he was featured in the article. You didn't get any mention," Paul reports.

"I still can't believe I didn't see him in the race. You might think I'm… weird for looking up his results. Sometimes I stay up almost 'til midnight looking stuff up.

"I would think it weird if you didn't. Everybody checks out their competition," Paul replies earnestly, leaning toward Eric.

That night, Eric relaxes at his desk reading the cross country message board. He finds some comments about Vance that get his attention. He reads a comment from someone with the screen name "Dirt Trail" who has typed:

> it looks like Vance might fulfill his promise.

The next comment, from "Nacho," reads:

> He was good last season until he got hurt.

After that, "I ♥ XC" has written:

> He's good but the rest of the Regal team sucks! After Vance, they got no one. I don't think they even have enough guys for a full team.

Eric shakes his head and turns off the computer. He picks up his biology book and gets into bed. He studies for a half an hour before falling asleep after a long day.

It's morning and the sun shines through the window onto Eric's face. He's sleeping with the same biology book beside him. He jolts awake and looks at the time. He forgot to set the alarm.

"Oh no—the biology test!" Eric exclaims. Even though he studied, he's nervous about the test. In panic mode, he dresses at double speed, shovels the books into his backpack, and hurries to school.

Eric barges into class late. He goes around to the back, trying not to be noticed, and sits. Mr. Lopez sees him and hands him a test.

"You're late," he says. Eric looks at the first two questions on the page and realizes he's in trouble.

Later, after school, Eric relaxes his pace as he returns to school at the end of a distance run. He cruises through the Regal field and finishes the run under the watchful eye of Coach Morris. Eric stops, bends forward, and puts his hands on his knees to recover.

"You can do better," Coach Morris says, looking at Eric. Eric walks off across the field.

"Where're you going? Hit the shower," Coach Morris says.

"Gonna do some wind sprints. For my speed."

"Eric, don't overdo it. Just do ten."

"Okay," Eric says before racing downfield. A surprised and pleased Coach Morris watches Eric complete a fast hundred-yard wind sprint out in the field alone.

A few minutes later, Paul runs onto the field. Not far behind are Katy, Ellie, and Grace. As they all finish their workout, they cluster around Coach Morris to recover. The girls walk into the locker room. Paul looks over and notices Eric sprinting downfield.

"Wind sprints," Coach Morris says, noticing Paul watching. "Why don't you get out there and join him?"

"Okay," Paul says, walking toward Eric.

Eric finishes another sprint and walks in a small circle to recover.

"How many was that?" Paul asks.

"Nine. One more."

"Perfect timing, I'll do the last one with you. Is Coach making you run these?"

"It's my idea. I want to work on my sprint speed. Did you read the cross country message board the other night?"

"I missed it."

"They basically said our whole team sucks, except for Vance."

Later that evening, Eric and Maria are in the Runners Sole store. This time Eric stands in front of assorted racing shoes. He recognizes the shoes Vance and Paul wear at the meets. Eric shows one to his mom. She bounces it in her hand to gauge the weight, then smiles. "I wish they'd made these when I was running," she says. Eric takes out two ten-dollar bills and tries to hand them to his surprised mom.

"Put your money away. This is my treat."

Before going to bed, Eric picks up one of the shoes, which are on his nightstand. He admires the overall design. After a moment, he gets up and gently places the shoe on his desk, beneath the medal on the wall. He looks at his video game controller for a moment. He turns on his computer, thinking a couple of games should be okay.

The early morning sun shines through the bedroom window on Eric. The sun awakens him. Eric is still sleepy as he tries to sit up. He looks over at his running shoes, then at the controller, and knows he was up way too late playing games. But the shoes, and the excitement of running his new out-and-back course, get him past a lazy moment. He decides he'd better start going to bed earlier to avoid groggy mornings like this.

Fifteen minutes later, Eric is stepping out onto the porch with the new racing shoes on. He figures he should try them out before a race. He jogs through the sleepy neighborhood on his way to El Paseo Road and the old city-limits sign. He's decided to try to beat his time from last week. He runs under the sign between the posts, starts the watch, and picks up the pace.

Out on the old highway, two kids on racing bikes leisurely pass him. He's feeling pretty good and decides to try and keep up with them. He starts to gain on them and soon can hear them talking and laughing. When the two riders hear Eric's shoes hitting the gravel behind them, they turn and see Eric getting closer. They look at each other and then rise from their seats to pedal faster and widen the gap on Eric, standing on the pedals. He accelerates again, briefly keeping up, then backs off to a reasonable pace, still feeling good. The shoes make him feel quick, like his feet weigh nothing.

The bikes pass through the Verdugo Road intersection as Eric continues to run hard to get there. He reaches his turnaround and looks at his watch: eighteen minutes even. Pleased, he turns around and is hit by a gust of wind. Eric is dismayed: The wind probably helped his time a lot on the way out, and now he's running against it. He puts his head down to fight through the stiff breeze, but it saps his energy and he really slows down. Discouraged and fatigued, Eric reaches the city-limit sign and stops his watch. He slows to look at the time—37:51. Surprised to discover that, despite being thwarted by the wind, he ran faster. Pleased, he jogs slowly home.

Thursday at school in biology class, Mr. Lopez hands out the graded test. Eric takes his sheaf of papers from the teacher and looks at the C-minus written on the first page. He isn't surprised. He makes a promise to study next time, but he's too excited about his new shoes to really care.

Arrow Park Double-Dual Meet

After school the cross country team assembles in the parking lot, near the van. Eric walks up to Paul and pulls his new shoes from his bag.

"Wow, new racing shoes!" Paul exclaims.

"You like them?" Eric asks.

"Yeah, they're perfect. I got the same thing," Paul says, looking at them. "You're hardcore now, man."

The coach yells out to the team. "Okay, listen up. Today is our second league meet, a double-dual, at Arrow Park. We should get there in a half-hour. We'll run against Rockford and Newark. Varsity, please remember to warm up for at least twenty minutes. Some of you are slacking off." He looks at the varsity boys. Mike, Barry, Taylor, and Kyle are all silent.

"You haven't won a race yet. Aren't you guys getting tired of losing?" Coach asks, looking around. "Let's go!"

The van pulls up to Arrow Park. The girls get out first, and then the boys.

Thirty minutes later, twenty-five runners are standing on the starting line for the frosh-soph boys' race. Eric and Paul stand between the much larger teams from Rockford and Newark. They focus their attention on the course ahead. An official tells them to take their positions and raises a starting pistol. Eric looks down at his new shoes. They feel good and give him confidence.

"Runners, take your marks!"

The boys crouch, one leg forward, eyes ahead.

"Runners *set—*"

The gun fires. In unison the boys take off, and Eric sprints to the front. He slows just long enough to position himself behind the leaders.

Five minutes later, Maria and Mr. Tate cluster near the trail as the runners near a bridge. Eric is right behind the leaders as they come into view. Paul reaches the bridge a minute after Eric, caught in the midst of a dense pack of other runners.

Coach Morris is on the canal path beyond the bridge and yells to Eric, "Put them in your mirrors!"

Perplexed, Eric looks back.

"*Pass 'em!*" Coach Morris yells.

Eric takes a deep breath and pushes his legs faster. He takes the lead as he crosses the bridge and continues on the path.

Coach Morris claps and cheers. "Come on!"

"Kid looks good," says the Rockford coach beside him.

"He's my new prodigy," Coach Morris replies.

Eric runs smoothly as he heads toward the finish with a sizable lead. Nearby, Vance has stopped jogging to watch Eric finish before he resumes his warm-up. Eric nears the finish and a sudden feeling of alarm comes over him. He wonders if anyone finished ahead of him. *Can't worry about that now—just get to the line.* The crowd erupts in cheers as Eric breaks the thin string stretched above the finish line. A female student meets him at the finish chute and removes the label from his singlet.

A few of the other freshmen runners congratulate Eric as they all walk slowly through the chute, breathing hard. He hesitantly compliments them in return. Eric exits the chute and is met by Coach Morris and Maria. Coach pats him on the back and Maria hugs him. Eric is still wondering.

"What place?" he asks.

"First," Coach and Maria say together.

"Really? I actually won this time?" Eric asks. Convinced at last, he slumps in relief. Then he turns back toward the finish. "I'm going to cheer for Paul."

He jogs back down along the course and sees Paul just behind a Rockford freshman. The other kid looks exhausted.

"You can pass that guy! Sprint now, Paul!" Eric yells. Paul goes into overdrive and darts past the other kid, who looks across in despair and tries to sprint with him. After a few steps, the Rockford kid gives up. Paul crosses the finish line ahead.

The following Monday afternoon, in the field behind the school, the atmosphere is noticeably different. Cross country practice is over for the boys' team—except Eric, who's doing wind sprints again, back and forth, while the varsity runners are heading toward the locker room. Mike and Barry stop to watch Eric run.

"Frickin' overachiever," Mike remarks.

"Yeah. We better get outta here before the coach makes us all do it. C'mon, let's play some pool," Barry says.

As they leave, Paul strides onto campus toward the finish of his run. He stops, then continues over to Eric's imaginary finish line on the field. Katy, Grace, and Ellie run by as Eric does another sprint across the grass. Eric looks up to see Ellie pass but quickly looks away again. He thinks briefly about talking to her, but he concentrates on the sprints first. He can't let his focus be distracted. He sprints back toward Paul, who's standing in the grass and shaking his head.

"C'mon, Paul," Eric says. Paul gives in and joins him. They sprint together. "I have a new course that I run," Eric says as they come to a stop.

"What is it?" Paul asks.

"I've been going down El Paseo Road to Verdugo Road and back."

"When do you run that?"

"On the weekends."

"You're running every day now?"

"I guess so. I've done it a couple of times. The first time I ran it I did thirty-eight fifty. The second time was against the wind, but I still improved to thirty-seven fifty-one."

"Wow, that's huge!"

"Thanks. And also for telling me about the racing shoes. They really help."

"Encouragement helps, too," Paul adds, nodding toward the girls.

The early morning quiet is shattered by the loud sound of a leaf blower. It wakes Eric up. He wipes the sleep out of his eyes. He's not excited to get up early to run anymore, but more important, he's not tired. So there's no excuse not to get up. He's following through on his plan of going to bed earlier, being consistent, to ensure that he gets enough sleep. He's well rested and ready to go. He gets up and picks out a pair of running shorts.

As Eric steps out onto the porch, ready to run, Maria looks out of her window and smiles. He checks the watch and starts jogging down the street toward the gardener with the leaf-blower. As Eric nears him, he shuts off the blower and the dust and leaves drop. Eric closes his eyes as he passes through the debris. Then the gardener turns his machine on again.

At the city limits sign, Eric runs between the posts and starts his watch. He gradually speeds up and settles on a pace. He watches the trees to gauge the wind. There doesn't seem to be a breeze, but Eric has a bounce to his stride as he lopes along the edge of the road. The wings on his feet are back.

Eric reaches the Verdugo Road intersection and checks the watch: 18:25. He makes the turn and heads back. There's no headwind at all. Eric feels comfortable and enjoys the run back, speeding up slightly before he reaches the city limit sign and clicks his watch. 36:37. He's knocked a minute and 14 seconds off, and he isn't even tired as he jogs home.

Crescenta Park Double-Dual Meet

The sun shines bright in the cloudless sky. A brown bar of smog, low across the sky, is visible in the distance. The windless day seems warmer than the actual temperature, but it's still a good day for Regal High's third league meet, another double dual, at Crescenta Park. Eric and Paul are at the starting line, surrounded again by bigger frosh-soph teams from the two other schools, Fitch and Wayland. The Regal teammates tap fists together to wish each other good luck and calm their nerves while they await the start. The ninth- and tenth-graders gather themselves, twenty-nine determined kids looking ahead at the same goal. The starter raises his hand.

"Runners, take your marks. Runners *set…*"

Maria and Mr. Tate wait at the one-mile mark amidst a crowd of spectators. A pack of runners turn a corner and approach, raising dust on the dry trail. The spectators clap and cheer.

Maria yells, "Go, Eric!"

Eric is in the lead. The path leading to a playground is a roar of sound as the runners begin a second loop. Eric looks back to check his lead. He is alone. He relaxes a bit to enjoy the race. He comes off a sharp turn onto the last straightaway more than a hundred meters ahead and sees Vance standing on the side of the course.

"Good job, Eric!" Vance yells. The shout electrifies Eric, who sprints full-out. *Wait 'til Paul hears that Vance yelled for me,*" he thinks. Looking ahead, he sees Coach Morris check his stopwatch. Eric focuses on the finish line and gives one last push for speed. He crosses the line and smiles broadly at Coach Morris, who is speechless. Eric jogs through the finish chute, then waits there and congratulates the next few runners coming in.

By late afternoon the teams are packing up. The spectators have already left, except for a few parents. The park is littered with streamers and signs as if a carnival has come and gone.

"Well, varsity, for anyone who cares, we lost both meets. Third out of three," Coach Morris tells his runners.

Mike, who is wearing his red **<17** shirt, stands and swings his duffle bag over his shoulder.

"We got third last year. At least we're consistent."

Coach Morris pulls a green T-shirt from a big gym bag, and everyone grows quiet. He tosses the shirt to Eric. Eric unfolds the shirt to find **<17** printed on the pocket.

"Eric, you're a sub-seventeen-minute cross country runner for three miles," Coach Morris says. "Something I started late last year, my incentive program. Congratulations."

The team claps briefly. Paul keeps clapping for a moment after the others have stopped, then drops his hands quickly. Eric can't help smiling at him.

Coach Morris reaches into the bag again and pulls out a green shirt. The varsity boys stare at it. Coach tosses it to Vance. "I've always hoped I'd get to give one of these out," Coach Morris says. "Vance, what can I say? That's not just a school record; it's the first sub-fifteen-minute three-mile in Royal High history."

Vance holds up his green **<15** shirt, and the whole team responds in awed, quiet voices: "Whoa…" "Sub-*fifteen*?"

"Jeez…" "Nice *job*, dude…" Vance places the shirt carefully in his bag. He doesn't say anything, but his face says it all.

Coach Morris turns to Eric, who's still gazing at his own shirt. "Great job today, Eric. All that extra effort is starting to pay off. You're next challenge is at Mount SAC."

What the heck is Mount Sack? Eric wonders.

The team finishes packing up and heads toward the parking lot, abuzz with talk about the T-shirts. When they reach the van, Paul and Eric see Vance get into a car parked nearby. Before shutting the door, he nods at Eric.

"Did you see that?" Eric says as Vance drives off.

"Sure did," Paul replies. "You just got acknowledged by one of the best runners in the state. Pretty good for a newbie."

"Yeah, and he cheered for me at the finish."

Behind them, Mike is causing a stir among the other varsity boys.

"Okay, Eric got the shirt," Mike says dramatically. "But just because he won this two-bit league meet doesn't mean he has a shot at Mount SAC."

"Yeah," agrees Rick, eating a candy bar. "He's going to need a lot more than a shirt to make it up the Switchbacks."

Coach Morris walks up beside them.

"How many races did you win last year?" Coach asks, looking at Mike.

"I ran varsity against Vance last year."

"That's a lame excuse. You should be challenging Vance," Coach says, shaking his head. "Stop wasting time and get in the van," he adds as Rick continues to eat the candy bar. The coach turns his attention to Rick.

"And you?" Coach says.

Rick stops chewing and swallows nervously. "Uh, no wins, Coach."

"How're the candy bar sales going?"

"Good, Coach," Rick says, before cautiously taking another bite.

"How many have you sold?"

Rick is hesitant. He starts calculating.

"Well?"

"Two boxes. Fifty dollars," Rick answers.

"What about the rest?"

"Huh?"

"You had three boxes to sell. What happened to the other box?" Coach asks.

"Umm…I ate them."

Coach slaps his clipboard, "You ate twenty-five candy bars?"

"I guess," Rick says meekly.

"Okay, you're off the job," Coach declares. "You owe the school twenty-five dollars. That's school property," he says, pointing to the candy bar in his hand. "Give it up."

Rick hands over the half-eaten bar reluctantly, knowing it's the last one he'll be eating for a while. The coach throws it into a trash can.

"You're eating our team's profits, and your diet is hurting your running. You obviously missed the point here, didn't you?"

"Yes, Coach," Rick says, looking down.

"Now, to make up the difference, you'll be working for me after school. That means clean the locker room, help me in the office, whatever I need. One week."

"What?" Rick says, shocked.

"And to burn off that candy, twenty-five push-ups daily for the week."

"But, Coach," Rick pleads.

"It's either that or I ask your parents for the twenty-five dollars," Coach says.

"No! I'll do the push-ups."

"And I want to see improvement in your running. I see you eating another candy bar, you're off the team."

Silence follows as Rick slinks into the back of the van and sits down. The other boys file in slowly. Coach Morris notices the somber mood.

"Toughen up, people. It'll get worse before it gets better," he says.

In the van, Eric trades his T-shirt for the new **<17** shirt and turns to Paul.

"What's Mount Sack?"

"S-A-C, for Mount San Antonio College. It's our next invitational meet. You mean you never heard of it?"

"No—what is it?"

"Nothing much. Sixteen thousand runners, six hundred schools, more than eighty races. Just the biggest high school cross country race in the whole country. You'll be running in front of thousands of people."

"Oh," Eric replies, smiling, in a mocking casual voice. "Not a big deal then."

"Nope," Paul says. "No big deal."

On Friday morning, the students walking to school are already thinking about the weekend. Eric and Paul are no different, but they're thinking about Mount SAC. They stop in front of the school to read the large digital ground sign before entering.

FOOTBALL SATURDAY

Home Game   Come cheer the team

Beat Hammond!

"Why don't they mention anything about Mount SAC?" Paul says.

"Maybe they don't think cross country is a sport. Like my dad thinks," Eric remarks. Paul rolls his eyes at him as they walk on.

In history class, Miss Anderson hands out graded test papers. As she hands Eric his test, he's shocked to see a large D in red ink on the top of the page. He looks up at her.

"I know you're better than this," she whispers before continuing to hand out papers. Eric feels like he got punched in the stomach. He's never gotten a D before.

Mount San Antonio Cross Country Invitational

It's early Saturday morning, the big day of the Mount SAC meet. Eric's alarm goes off and he perks up. He grabs his clothes and racing shoes and places them in his gym bag. His mom is making toast and waiting for him in the kitchen.

"Good morning, Eric. Sit down, breakfast is almost ready."

"I'm not eating. I'm just taking some chips and juice with me for later."

"You need food to race three miles. The key is to eat light. I'm making you some wheat toast. Sit down," she says, pouring him some orange juice. Eric gives in and sits down at the table.

"Mount SAC," His mom says. "I remember every bit of that course. I can't believe my own son will be running it twenty years later." The toast pops up, and she sets it on Eric's plate. He butters a slice and begins to eat.

"Is the course as tough as they say?" Eric asks between bites.

"Yes, but if you're ready, you can attack it. Don't go out too fast. The race really starts at the first hill—and it gets tough. There are three big hills, with long downhills in between." Eric listens intently while chewing his toast.

"There are lots of people in each race, so it's crowded. Just concentrate on the course and focus on what's in front of you. You'll pass people in the second half if you run smart," she says. "Do you want to ride with me up there?"

"Mom, you know the rules. I have to ride with the team, even if you are a state champion," Eric says. He's done eating and stands up. His mom gives him a hug.

"Mom!" Eric says, squirming.

She lets him go, and he finishes his juice.

"I'll see you there," he says as he picks up his bag getting ready to go. His mom gives him a final hug, and he gives in.

"I'm proud of you son," Maria says, ruffling his hair.

"Mom! I gotta go," Eric declares, rushing out. "See ya later."

"I'll see you there," she says before the door closes. Dale walks in, yawning.

"Was that Eric leaving already?" he asks.

"He's got a big race today."

"On a Saturday?"

"I'm going to watch him. Why don't you come?"

"I have a lot to do today. That's why I'm up early."

"If he was in a football game, you'd be there," she says somberly. Dale pours a cup of coffee.

"We'll see. If I have time," he says and walks out of the kitchen. Maria sighs in frustration.

The Regal High School van pulls into the large Mount San Antonio College parking lot. Behind it, the Leigh High School buses stretch down the road. Leigh is a cross country powerhouse, with fast individuals and lots of boys and girls ready to replace them if they falter. Leigh has A, B, and C teams of Varsity runners. While Regal cross country isn't on anyone's radar, Leigh's successful team is known everywhere. With a good distance coach, Leigh has a history of state championships in cross country and track. When they pull into the parking lot, their buses take up five parking spaces and not a single seat looks empty.

"Here's Leigh and its army," Mike says as they watch the huge team leave the buses.

"Wonder if they'll lose any of the divisions this year?" Barry says.

"They probably have people here just to carry the trophies home," Taylor adds.

"Knock it off—stop acting like losers," Vance scoffs.

Without instruction, the Leigh team splits up into separate groups—varsity, junior varsity, and freshmen. At the coach's signal, they all jog forward in unison past the Regal High team, looking more like an ROTC squad than a cross country team.

"They have some good runners," Paul says apprehensively.

"Don't let them scare you," Coach Morris replies.

"They're the defending state champs. Travis is their top returning guy," Paul says.

"They have three guys back from last year's team," Vance adds.

"They're only as good as their fifth man," Coach says.

"What's the big deal?" Mike replies. "It's not like we're going to win a team medal or anything. The only guy who has a chance to win is you, Vance,"

Coach interrupts: "If you feel like you have no chance, then you might as well quit now," he says.

Mike is silent.

"Now let's get ready to race—and do your best," Coach says.

The team walks to a big field where each school has been assigned a spot to make a camp. Regal's team sets up near the river embankment, close to another school that far outnumbers them. Some of the varsity boys take off their sweats and go for a warmup run. Rick, hiding from Coach beside Paul, hastily finishes a candy bar as Paul and Eric pin on their race numbers. Paul looks curiously at Rick.

"Not a word to Coach," he warns, his mouth full of chocolate.

"Don't worry—I was just wondering: How can you eat that just before a race? Doesn't your stomach bother you?"

"Not from eating. It only hurts when I go out too fast. Coach can't expect a guy to go cold turkey."

"Okay, varsity boys," says Coach. "Get going to the starting line. Eric. Paul. You should think about warming up."

Eric's and Paul's race isn't for another half-hour, so they decide to hit the port-a-johns before joining the other spectators to watch the first race. At least thirty people wait in line near the edge of the park where the port-a-johns are set up.

"I can wait," Eric decides.

"I'm gonna stick it out," Paul replies. "Looks like the line is moving a little. See you in a bit."

Eric jogs back over to the race course to watch the varsity race, which has already begun. He's overwhelmed by the numbers of spectators and runners lining the course at the Corridor, where the runners reappear after they've climbed course's toughest hill, the Switchbacks. He manages to work his way through the crowd to get near the race. He's nervous about the crowd, but he gets excited when they begin to scream as the runners come down from the switchbacks and into view. Two Leigh runners lead, with Vance close behind. They pass through the Corridor, packed three rows deep with frenzied spectators greeting them across the halfway point, just a few feet from Eric. After the first ten runners pass, the crowd begins to thin out as fans rush to another part of the course to see the leaders climb the next hill and then approach the finish. In a few seconds, Eric is alone watching the stragglers. He walks to the northern corner of the course, where Paul catches up. As they meet, a crowd begins to accumulate excitedly waiting for the runners to appear again.

"What have I missed?" Paul asks.

"Two Leigh runners had the lead going up the last hill and Vance was right behind them. They should be coming down this hill soon."

"This is a critical spot. Once they pass this corner there's only four hundred meters to go," Paul says.

They keep their eyes on the bend in the trail as others crowd around them to get a better view. Suddenly applause erupts as the runners round the bend. A Leigh runner appears—and then Vance, about thirty meters back. The next Leigh runner is now a distant third.

"That's Travis in the lead. Vance's competition," Paul says.

Travis races past, followed by Vance. *"Come on, Vance!"* Eric and Paul shout in unison. The runners are both sprinting full-out, and the gap between them stays the same as they race returning down the old paved road known as the "airstrip," passing the start and then turning right, and into a spectator-lined short finish strip with a brief incline 15 meters from the finish line. The second Leigh man crosses the line, and then a steadily thickening stream of varsity boys follows. The other Regal boys are in the thick of the flow: Mike is the team's second finisher, followed closely by Taylor, Barry, and Kyle. Rick trails in near the back of the field. As the crowd begins to disperse, Paul checks his watch. "We better go get ready," he says.

"Are you nervous?" Eric asks.

"Yeah, a little. You?"

"Yeah. A little, with all these people around," Eric says.

The last of the runners pass by and the airstrip opens up. Paul and Eric walk toward the start. Coach Morris approaches them.

"Okay, you two. In a race like today's, you have to get out fast in the first hundred meters, near the front, before the first turn or you'll be stuck in the back. The trail narrows and has a lot of sharp turns. In a big pack like you have here, once you're behind, it's hard to get past people and move up. You follow me?"

They both nod.

"It's for races like this that you're doing wind sprints," Coach says.

After a few short strides for a warmup, they join a crowd of about 250 freshman runners at the starting line. Leigh's uniforms, brown with orange trim, are dominant; some are faded, older styles representing past varsity attire because the team is too large for everyone to get a new one. Eric looks around, feeling lost in the big crowd. This is the biggest race he's ever been in. Because Eric and Paul are small even for freshmen, they get swallowed in the group of taller runners. They worm their way to the front of the starting line. Eric nervously adjusts his shirt, bends forward to stretch his legs, and takes a deep breath. Beads of sweat appear on his forehead. He thinks, *It's only a race, just calm your nerves.* He looks at Paul, who appears focused. Paul notices Eric looking at him. Paul holds out his fist. Eric looks down and they tap their knuckles together.

"Don't be nervous. I'm right behind you," Paul says.

"Okay," Eric says, looking forward, still concerned. *It's only a race.* If he just looks straight ahead he can concentrate. He remembers his mom's words—*get into the zone, just focus on what's in front of you.* Suddenly, he turns and sees his mom in the crowd, looking at him and smiling. He focuses back on the race. Eric can't help but notice that next to him is a large shoulder. He looks up at the boy beside him. He has flourishing facial hair and looks like he's in college, not Leigh High School. Eric feels intimidated. He looks away when the taller runner turns to look at him.

"Good luck," the Leigh runner says.

"Yeah, good luck," Eric replies, glancing back before staring straight ahead. He looks past the airstrip, to the dirt trail, at the first turn, 300 meters ahead. He leans forward into starting position, left foot in front, arms dangling at his sides. He raises his head, getting poised while watching the official raise the starting gun… and it fires! Immediately Eric and Paul get hit by elbows as runners crowd them, jockeying for position along the airstrip. They reach the dirt trail before the first turn and scramble to keep their position. Eric speeds up and manages to get near the front as the runners converge at the first turn. A few feet back, Paul, not quick enough, is swallowed by the main group.

Entering the Valley Loop, the path narrows and the runners squeeze closer together to run the first of the two half-mile loops. After the second loop, Eric is just behind the lead pack. They reach the first mile marker. Eric's legs feel good; he's surprised that he's already run a mile. It seemed to take two minutes.

After the flat first mile, the runners reach the Switchbacks: 380 meters of steep uphill around four hairpin turns. As he climbs, working now but not tiring, Eric notices the older looking Leigh competitor right in front of him, laboring and slowing down.

Eric passes the Leigh runner without speeding up, pacing himself up the hill, conserving energy. After the relief of reaching the crest, he picks up the pace as the trail becomes a long, sweeping downhill.

Eric doesn't sprint on the next subtle downhill in the Corridor, but the older-looking Leigh runner does and catches up to him. They run together between the walls of screaming fans. Eric is too worried about being passed to notice the spectators. He runs toward "Poop Out Hill," so named because so many runners

tire out on it. The Leigh runner passes Eric on the beginning of the arduous climb to the cheers of a crowd of fans lined up along the hillside. Most of the spectators encourage the runners while others are there to watch the pain. Halfway up, Eric catches him again; the larger boy is struggling on this climb, too. Eric speeds up, crests the 300-meter hill, and charges down the short downhill on the other side. As the trail levels out, he looks back: he has a twenty-meter gap on his Leigh rival. He turns his attention ahead, noticing how quiet it is on the other side of the hill, away from the crowd. He's gaining on the lead pack of four runners; three are also from Leigh High. With a bold move, he shifts to the right and presses past the group. A flood of adrenaline hits him. *I'm leading! Did I go too soon?* he thinks. Two Leigh runners manage to keep up with him, but the other two boys fall behind. The lead group of three races across a flat 400-meter section and reach the third and final climb—Reservoir Hill—together.

They all attack the hill, named for the reservoir water tanks at the top. One Leigh runner, a slender blond kid whose brown singlet flaps on his small shoulders, opens a slight gap on Eric, who struggles to maintain contact. When they've climbed for about 250 meters, they reach a brief plateau. Eric uses the flat section to throw in a surge, and the gap on the leader closes. Eric looks up: there's another twenty meters of hill still to go. He's already committed himself, so he grimaces and pushes on. With his legs burning, he catches the leader at the top of the hill and, keeping his momentum, passes him as they begin the descent. Eric opens up his stride and lets the gravity do the work. Halfway down, he senses that his rival is no longer on his heels. He freewheels out onto the flat and reaches Norton's Corner. He risks a glance back to check his lead. Elation and relief fill him as he sees the thin Leigh runner thirty meters back, struggling. Eric feels strong and confident about the last 400 meters. He makes the turn down the finish gauntlet, which is one hundred and fifty meters long. The crowd noise is overwhelming and everything seems to slow down. Eric sees Ellie, Grace, and Katy, with huge smiles on their faces, standing in a row along the fence near the finish. He manages to smile back, and they shriek his name happily, pumping their fists. The large crowd is exploding with applause. As he struggles over the last agonizing little rise to reach the line he feels like he's running in slow motion and will never reach it. When he's a step away, as if to confirm that he isn't dreaming, he hears the race announcer over the loudspeaker:

"It looks like our freshman champion is Eric Hunt from Regal High!"

Eric pumps his fist into the air and crosses the finish line. He slows to a walk and turns around to see how far behind the other runners are. He watches as two Leigh runners sprint in a battle for second place about ten seconds behind him. An official ushers him forward through the finish chute. Looking around, he spots his mom and Mr. Tate just past the announcer's booth, both clapping wildly, huge smiles on their faces. Walking through the chute, someone claps a hand on Eric's shoulder. Eric turns and is surprised to see that it's the older-looking kid, who has fought back to edge his teammate for second. He waits in the chute and extends a hand. The Leigh runner catches up and grabs it.

"Hey, good race, man," says the tall kid, catching his breath. "Greg Miller."

"Eric Hunt."

"First time at Mount SAC?"

"Yup."

"Me, too. I wasn't sure how I'd handle it—bigger guys are supposed to have trouble on hills."

"You did pretty well, I'd say."

"Thanks. Some people hassle me because I look too big to be a freshman."

"Whoa. I don't quite have that problem."

"I'm comin' after you next time we race," Greg says, smiling.

"You're on."

Eric walks out of the finish chute and waits there as other runners stagger through. He sees Paul nip past two other boys just before the finish. Eric waits as Paul walks through the crowded chute. Paul looks up and sees Eric waiting for him, and smiles.

"How'd you do?" Paul asks, out of breath.

"I can't believe it. First," Eric says, beaming.

"You got first? That's awesome!"

"How was your race?"

"Not bad, not great—seventy-fourth. I died on the hills, but I had a pretty good kick. Those wind sprints really help."

A passing photographer stops to snap Eric's picture. The photographer moves on as Eric and Paul look at each other open-mouthed.

"All *right!*" Paul says, "I knew you could do it."

They high-five each other.

After Paul and Eric have taken a cooldown jog, they walk past the official results board. There are several pages for each race. Runners and coaches cluster around the board in a dense mass, trying to find their results in the columns of hundreds of names and times.

"Hey, our results might be up. Let's check it out," Paul says.

They snake their way through the crowd, their small size an advantage for once. They maneuver to the front, close to the board. They scan the pages.

"Here we are," Paul exclaims. "Your name's easy to find." Another page stapled near their race results lists the course records and all-time top performers. "Look at that... wow, your time puts you *fifth* on the all-time list for freshmen on this course!"

Eric moves in to see. There's his name, in first place. He looks at the all-time list. It's true—only four times are faster than 15:36, the time that he just ran.

"Geez," Paul says. Eric looks over at him.

"Oh, man. I'm on the second page," Paul groans, running his finger down a column of names.

"It's almost time for the awards ceremony," Eric says.

"You go ahead—I'll catch up."

"Okay. Don't be late,"

Eric weaves his way out of the crowd. Paul looks back up at the board and scans the other race results. One catches his attention: their varsity boys' race. Paul sees Vance's name in second place, then his school and his grade, 12, listed before the finishing time. Paul glances down the grade column and notices a single digit standing out among the 12's and some 11's. It's a 9—a freshman. Paul traces backwards to the name: Todd Bryce, in sixth place. Paul is amazed when he reads the finish time: 15:23. He turns around, but Eric is long gone. Paul looks back and takes a few moments to memorize Bryce's result, then winds his way out.

Twenty minutes later, Eric is standing on the top of a podium accepting his award. An official walks toward the podium, and Eric bends forward to let him place a ribbon with a gold medal around his neck. The small crowd claps for the five award winners. Eric and the other four boys congratulate one another. Wearing his first individual award, Eric looks up with pride. He sees Coach Morris, Maria, and Paul clapping as well. Eric wonders if his dad would be clapping for him.

As the Regal team packs up, the varsity clusters together to discuss the day's events.

"You see that freshman win the race?" Taylor asks, jerking a thumb toward Eric.

"Freshman? What are you, nuts? Who cares about a freshman?" Mike says.

"I guess you're jealous that he won," Taylor replies. "And, here he is."

Mike turns and frowns as Eric approaches. Ellie walks over to Eric.

"Congratulations, Eric," Ellie says. "You ran a fantastic race."

"Thanks, Ellie," Eric says shyly.

The entire team converges around Eric, offering congratulations as Mike watches.

"Way to go, freshman," Mike says under his breath.

"Good job," says Vance. "I never won here as a freshman."

As Vance leaves, Eric looks over at Paul.

"Did you hear that?"

Paul nods. "I saw it. Vance actually talked to you. You, a freshman."

"I guess we have the fastest freshman in the state," Taylor says, slapping Eric hard on the back.

"Not quite," Paul replies. Eric's smile fades a little as he looks over at Paul, who continues, "I saw the varsity results. Skyline has a freshman on varsity named Bryce. His time was thirteen seconds faster."

Eric stares at him. "What? He ran varsity?" He walks off to look at the results.

"A freshman? What place was he?" Mike asks.

"Sixth."

"Sixth? Crap. He beat me," Mike replies.

"That's not the bad news," Barry says.

Mike looks at him, annoyed. "What's the big bad news, then?"

"Eric beat your time."

Mike's face goes slack. Then he says, "Beginner's luck."

Coach Morris walks over to the group and sees Eric walking away. "Eric, get back here!" he yells. Eric makes an about-face and comes back. "Congratulations," Coach announces to the team. "Eric just made varsity."

Mike falls over, pretending to have a heart attack. Maria beams at Eric.

"Congratulations, Eric," she says proudly. Paul elbows Eric to get his attention.

"What a coincidence," says Paul. "Bryce runs varsity, too."

"No kidding," says Eric, hiding a smile.

"Come on over to my house for dinner," Paul says to Eric. "We'll look up your stats."

"Hey, Mom, Paul invited me over for dinner. Can I hang out for a few hours when we get back?"

"As long as you're home before nine."

"Thanks, Mom."

Paul's bedroom is adorned with running paraphernalia: race numbers, pace charts, magazine covers of runners, and a few finishing photos of himself. Eric and Paul, still in their sweats, are on the computer. Eric still has his medal around his neck.

"Hey, look," Paul says. "The results are already up for today's race." Eric pulls his chair closer and eagerly looks at the screen.

"That's me!" Eric says excitedly, pointing at a photo.

"Wow, you got your picture up on the web," Paul says enthusiastically. Suddenly, the door bursts open.

Vanetta and Ellie look in.

"Mom's getting pizza. What do you guys want on it?" Vanetta asks.

"Hey, look, Eric has his picture online," Paul says.

"Big deal," Vanetta says. Ellie pokes her head in.

"I wanna see," Ellie exclaims. She goes up to Eric and Paul to see the computer. Eric shyly gets up and lets her have his seat. Ellie looks at the picture proudly.

She reads the caption under the photo: "Freshman Race Winner."

Vanetta leans on the doorjamb, feigning extreme boredom. The picture shows Eric crossing the finish line. Ellie turns to Eric.

"Can I see your medal?"

Eric takes it off from around his neck and hands it to her. She looks at it and smiles.

"Nice."

Eric smiles. "Thanks."

"These medals are better than the ones we got at cheerleading camp," Ellie says, holding it up for Vanetta to see.

Vanetta takes a casual glance.

"Yeah, I guess," Vanetta says, "C'mon, let's go back to my room."

"Give him some slack. He won a race," Paul says.

"Shut up, sweat bag," Vanetta snaps. "You need to take a shower—use soap this time!"

Ellie hands the medal back to Eric.

Paul blurts out, "Pepperoni! I'll have pepperoni on my pizza."

"Me too!" Eric calls.

The girls leave and the boys high five each other.

Later that night, Eric walks into his living room. Maria peeks in from the kitchen.

"Oh, you're home. How was Paul's?"

"It was great. We had pizza."

"That's nice. I'll be out in a minute. I'm finishing up the dishes." Eric hangs his medal on a hook over the fireplace. He steps back to look at it from all sides and practically dances around it with excitement. Dale enters the living room.

"What's this?" he asks, noticing the medal.

"That's what I won today," Eric says.

"Well, I guess you did better than thirty-fourth." He looks at it, unimpressed.

"I wish you could have been there today, Dad," Eric confesses. His mom comes out of the kitchen to see them both.

"Okay, Eric, time to clean up and get changed for bed."

"Mom, I got my picture on the internet for winning the race today," Eric says, walking up to her.

"That's nice, dear. Maybe your father and I can look at it later," she says, looking at him. He doesn't respond.

"Uh, sure, maybe later," Dale says.

Eric knows that if his dad sees it, it'll be because his mom forces him to.

"Now, go get some rest. You've had a long day."

"Okay, Mom," Eric says, heading toward his room. He leaves the door open and listens to his parents talking.

"The coach announced to the team today that Eric's being promoted to varsity," Maria says.

"Varsity?" Dale asks, doubt in his voice. "He's varsity?"

"Yes. What's wrong?"

"Freshmen don't just waltz onto varsity in a real sport. That's what I've been saying—running's just exercising, like to keep from getting fat. It's not a real sport."

"Eric didn't just 'waltz onto varsity.' He earned it. You should be proud of your son," Maria says sternly.

"It's not that I'm not proud. It just seems like a waste."

"Why?"

"Come on. It's just running around in circles. In real sports they use running for punishment."

"It *is* a real sport, Dale! It was my sport, too, and I have medals to show for it," Maria says getting annoyed.

"And what did it get you? It's not like football or basketball, where you can get a scholarship."

"That's not true—they do give scholarships for running. The sport *is* real, just because you don't recognize it as one. You want our son to be happy, don't you?"

"Yes, I do, but…"

"But what?" she presses.

"I want him to succeed."

"Me, too. He's old enough to make his own choice and running is something he enjoys," she says. "He's good at it," she adds more calmly.

"He'd be better off even playing golf," Dale mutters. "Those guys make a fortune." Eric hears him flop down on the couch.

Eric quietly closes his bedroom door. He stares into the room for a minute, unseeing. Then he notices his video-game controller, and picks it up.

The next Monday, at the back of the school, Eric is in biology class and having trouble with a test. He struggles with every question, resorting to guessing on most of them. He realizes that he should have studied more; he'd been caught up in the excitement of Mount SAC, reading everything he could find about the race and Bryce. By the time he opened a book, it was too late.

Later that afternoon behind the school, the cross country team is waiting around, ready to start practice. They're all listening to Barry reading from an article that he printed out from the internet about favorites to win the state cross country championships,

"Can you believe Travis from Leigh is rated number one? Vance got his picture on the internet for most improved. I don't care what anyone says," Barry tells Vance, "This is your year to win."

"That's what I'm talking about, boy," says Mike.

Taylor pretends to hold a microphone toward Vance, like a reporter. "To what do you attribute this year's vast improvement?"

Vance plays along. "Well, after some minor successes on the track, I felt that I had a future in the sport, so I made gigantic sacrifices. I put away the surfboard, the boogie-board, *and* the skateboard, and I hooked up with this serious training group over the summer. We really piled on the miles."

"Ah. You mention a training group. Are you referring to your distinguished teammates?" Taylor asks.

"I wish. My training group is made up of me, myself, and I," Vance says.

Everyone laughs.

"You guys are funny, even though I have *no* idea what you're talking about," Rick says.

"I dub thee 'National,'" Mike says to Vance. "That's *Mister* National to you freshmen," he says, pointing at Eric and Paul.

"Did anyone see Eric's picture?" Paul asks the group.

"I did," Vance replies. "Not bad, kid."

"I didn't see it," Mike cuts in. "Freshmen don't count."

"Better keep it to yourself," whispers Rick as Coach Morris approaches, carrying a piece of clothing folded in his hand.

"I hope you're all warmed up before I send you to run the Kenneth Street seven-mile loop," Coach says. He throws the piece of clothing to Eric, who catches it. He unfolds a varsity uniform singlet.

"You mean that was for real?" Mike says. The girls gather around Eric to congratulate him.

Eric triumphantly holds up his new singlet as Paul softly elbows Mike. Mike propels Paul away from him. Taylor, Mike, and Barry exchange unimpressed glances.

"Varsity, watch out. It's open season," Paul warns. Mike gives him an angry look, and Paul's smile fades. He moves away from Mike.

"Now, just because you got that uniform doesn't mean you can coast, Eric," Coach Morris tells him. "This is only the beginning."

"I know, Coach," Eric says, trying it on for size over his T-shirt. It's slightly large on his small frame, but he looks down, admiring it. "Coach, can I go put this in my locker?" he asks.

"Sure, I'll let you in. Let's go. And then you'll be running with the varsity team," he says. They walk off.

At his locker, Eric takes a long look at the varsity uniform, trying to absorb all that it represents. It's just a shirt, but it carries a lot of weight.

Outside, the girls take off running. Mike watches them and turns toward the team.

"Okay, let's go," Mike orders.

"Shouldn't we wait for Eric?" Kyle asks.

"Naw. He'll catch up. Didn't you hear, he's a varsity runner now."

The team starts to move except for Vance and Paul. Mike notices Vance not moving.

"Vance, aren't you coming?" Mike asks.

"You go ahead. I'll wait," Vance says. Paul hides his enjoyment as the rest of the team leaves.

Eric jogs excitedly out of the locker area, then stops in his tracks. Paul waits for him outside the building.

"Those guys left. They didn't want to stay around," Paul says.

"Thanks for waiting," Eric says, downcast. They walk toward the field. As they get closer to the grass, they see one team member warming up and coming over to them. It's Vance. Eric is surprised as Vance nears. Paul is all smiles.

"Vance waited," Paul says proudly.

"Are you ready to run?" Vance says as he comes to a stop.

"It would be an honor to run with you," Eric says enthusiastically.

"Me too!" Paul adds. Vance looks at Eric.

"Don't let it bother you. Everyone goes through it. I never got any respect until I was a junior."

"Okay," Eric says.

"Let's go!" Vance says.

"Yeah, let's go kick their butts!" Paul says. Eric and Vance look quizzically at him.

"I mean, let's go catch the other guys," Paul says. They begin to run through the field. Eric knows he should be thrilled about the progress he has made, but he still feels like an outsider.

As they leave the campus, Vance immediately starts to pull away. Eric looks at Paul.

"Don't even think about waiting for me," Paul tells him.

Eric smiles, slaps Paul on the back, and picks up the pace.

Out on the road, Eric manages to keep Vance in sight. Just over one hundred meters separates them. Up ahead, Vance passes Katy, Grace, and Ellie, and they cheer him on. A little while later the girls are surprised to see Eric pass by and they cheer wildly for him. Ellie claps and smiles and Eric smiles back.

"Way to go, varsity! Whoo-hoo!" the girls yell. Eric sheepishly acknowledges them and returns his focus on Vance up ahead. He thrusts his fist into the air as he accelerates.

Vance has disappeared up ahead. Eric runs through the park heading back to campus alone. He really needs to make a pit stop, so when he sees the community center, he changes course and runs through the front door of the building. Looking for a restroom, he unintentionally jogs into the game room. He stops in surprise. Mike and Barry are there, in their running clothes, playing a serious game of pool with some other guys. They all look up at Eric.

"No freshmen allowed!" Mike growls, walking toward Eric with a threatening look, pool cue in hand.

"I just need to use the bathroom," Eric says meekly. Now Barry is standing over him too.

"You say *one word* to Coach…" Mike says.

"I won't."

Mike lifts his chin, gesturing toward the bathroom, then he and Barry step aside and let him pass.

Moments later, Eric rushes back out without looking at them. Mike and Barry laugh and continue with their game as they watch Eric race out the door to finish the run.

Eric gets home after practice and walks into the entryway. He takes off his jacket to reveal the varsity singlet underneath. He looks at himself in the oval mirror on the wall and admires the screaming eagle head and color bars on his new racing top. A red bar below the head has the word "CROSS" printed on it. Just below that is the blue bar with "COUNTRY" on it. He stands proudly and smoothes the wrinkles out. He notices the fine texture of the lightweight micro-mini-mesh fabric sliding comfortably over his body. He marvels at the science behind the material and feels honored to be wearing something that can maximize his performance. He breathes in and puffs his chest out. Adrenaline surges through his body as he looks at himself in the mirror. He raises his arms up into a running position and breathes out.

Energized, he starts to swing his arms while standing in front of the mirror. He envisions himself mid-race near the front and ready to assert some authority. He puts his head down and surges up to the front pack. Sustaining his speed, he breaks away from the field. Nothing can stop him now as he races toward the finish line. He's so focused he doesn't even notice his dad come into the room and step in behind him.

"What's going on?" Dale asks, staring at his son, who's flailing his arms back and forth. Eric jolts back to reality and looks at his father. In the mirror he sees an aligned, portrait-like picture of father and son.

"I just got my varsity uniform singlet," Eric says to his dad in the mirror. He turns around to show it to him.

Dale looks it over, "Doesn't it even have a number, like a real jersey?"

Eric doesn't say anything.

"Son, with your speed, you could be running down a football field," Dale says. He walks out of the room, leaving Eric alone and discouraged. Eric walks away from the mirror and goes to his room.

The next day, Eric is trying to take his history test. He looks up to see the clock, and some movement in the hall catches his attention. Beef is at the tiny glass panel of the classroom door staring at him as if he's the only one in the classroom. Eric's concentration on the test is lost. Even though he studied over the weekend after getting a D on the last test, he has trouble focusing.

"You," Beef mouths. He clenches a fist where Eric can see it, then pounds it into the palm of his other hand.

Eric looks back down, trying to focus on the test. His attention alternates between answering questions on the page to glancing up at Beef mouthing profanities from behind the window.

Suddenly, the bell rings and Eric looks at the clock.

"Oh, no," Eric mutters. He's not done. He turns his test over in frustration and looks up. The window is empty, but he knows Beef could be close. The test papers are collected and students begin to walk out of the room. Eric stays inside, mingling with students near the door, wary of Beef. He carefully peers out and sees Beef hiding behind the door. Eric lets two students exit, then bolts through the doorway. With the students in Beef's way, Eric runs down the hall and reaches the stairs. Beef clumsily gets around the students and rushes down the hall after Eric. He tries to follow Eric down the stairs, but his size and momentum carry him past the top step. He tries to change direction but crashes into the wall, loses traction, and sprawls face-down at the top of the stairway. Nearby students laugh at him. Eric comes back up a few steps to see.

"I'm gonna get you!" Beef pants, struggling to his feet. "This ain't over!"

Most of the students continue to laugh at Beef. Eric jogs down the steps, laughing to himself.

It's a cool morning as Eric steps out onto the porch. He walks down the steps and starts to jog down the street toward El Paseo Road. He reaches the city limit sign and runs underneath it, clicking his stopwatch as he picks up the pace sharply. Traffic is light today on the old highway. A bicyclist going the opposite direction glances over at Eric as he cruises by across the road. Eric arrives at the isolated intersection at Verdugo Road. He looks at his watch, which reads 18:03 and turns back. Nearing the finish, he imagines he's racing Bryce and sprints to the sign. He runs under it, legs and lungs burning, and stops his watch. Slowing to a jog, he looks at the time: 35:59. He pumps his fist.

Coach Morris is driving the school van with Ellie, Kyle, Grace, Katy and Paul to Crescenta Park for a workout.

"Hey, Coach, can Eric be considered for captain?" Paul asks.

"Captains are elected. A lot of guys aren't going to vote for a freshman."

"Hey, there he is!" Ellie shouts out. They're catching up to Eric, who's running to the park on the side of the road.

"Coach, slow down," says Paul.

The coach slows down and honks as the van pulls alongside Eric. Eric glances over and waves to them.

"Hey, Coach, how fast is he going?" asks Paul. All the team members except Kyle move over to the windows.

"We'll just see," Coach says, slowing the van to Eric's pace.

"Hey, Eric, we're clocking your speed!" Paul shouts out.

Eric opens up his stride while the coach gradually applies the gas.

"He's doing over ten miles per hour now," says the coach.

"C'mon, Eric! You can beat this hunk-of-junk van that can't even go up hills!" yells Paul.

"Hey," says Coach Morris.

"Oh, sorry, Coach. I'm just trying to psych Eric up, that's all," Paul says. "Go, Eric!"

"Eleven miles per hour… twelve," says Coach. Everybody tries to see the speedometer. The van nears Eric's speed.

"Twelve miles an hour!" Paul yells to Eric. Eric waves and plays along. He faces straight ahead, grimacing as he quickens his stride.

"Go, Eric!" Ellie blurts out the window.

"Thirteen miles per hour!" Coach announces. The van is keeping up with Eric.

"Thirteen, Eric! Whoo-hoo!" yells Paul. Eric is in full flight but not quite sprinting as the van accelerates to stay next to him. The team is completely absorbed in Eric's running.

"Just over thirteen miles per hour," says a surprised Coach as he matches Eric's pace.

"Over thirteen miles an hour, Eric!" yells Paul. Eric bursts into a sprint and gets ahead of the van. The passengers go wild with cheers—all but Kyle, who looks uninterested. Ellie watches Eric, impressed with his speed. She's never watched a runner for

so long from so close up. She can see the way that Eric's feet plant firmly for a split second apiece and then keep him flying forward. Eric signals that he's done and slows to a jog. Coach Morris drives on ahead; Ellie, Grace, Katy, and Paul stick their heads out the windows and cheer as they leave a fatigued but smiling Eric behind on the roadside.

"He's going to need a new pair of shoes," Ellie says.

Coach Morris looks in his rear-view mirror. "He won't be elected captain, but he might earn a varsity letter."

Peninsula Double-Dual Meet

The Regal team arrives at Peninsula Park for its fourth and last league meet before League Finals. The opponents are Hammond and Fitch. The grounds are again full of parents and fans wearing team colors and shouting along the course. The air is full of energy and excitement. No one is taking in the atmosphere more fully than Eric. He's nervous but excited to be wearing the varsity uniform under his sweats. The girls' race is in progress as Eric and Paul stop at the trail. Eric watches as the girls approach. Katy is leading the second pack. Paul and Eric wait for her to get nearer.

"Go, Katy!" Eric and Paul shout in unison.

A few more runners pass, then Grace, with Ellie close behind.

"Come on, Grace!" Eric and Paul yell. Paul claps loudly. Standing nearby watching are two older Hammond runners, juniors or seniors. They notice Ellie coming.

"Come on, Ellie!" Paul shouts. The two Hammond kids pick up on the shouts and gradually move closer to Eric and Paul.

"Go, Ellie!" Eric yells.

"Come on Ellie!" Paul shouts.

"Doing great, Ellie!" shouts one Hammond boy, watching appreciatively as Ellie runs by. Paul and Eric turn to look at the Hammond boys.

"She's a babe," one says, turning to Paul and Eric. "Ellie, huh? Thanks for the introduction. I'm transferring to Regal," he says.

"She's not your type," Paul says as he and Eric walk away sharing a laugh.

When the race is finished, Eric and Paul leave the field and head toward a cluster of trees where the races start. The varsity boys' race is next.

"Aren't you going to finish warming up?" Paul asks.

"I'm warmed up. I feel pretty good, considering I'm running varsity. I don't even have to pee."

"Uh-oh," Paul replies. "Remember last time, you were feeling so good and you went out too fast."

"Yeah, but this time I'm starting out with Vance."

Paul looks at him in shock.

"I'm just kidding," Eric says. "I'll go out easy. I remember. It's a hilly course. I won't forget. I'll see you after the race."

On the starting line, Mike and Eric stand beside each other behind Vance. Mike glares at Eric like he doesn't belong. He steps in front of Eric to get a better position and squeezes into the front row next to Vance. The gun fires.

Eric doesn't sprint out ahead; instead, he conserves his energy, allowing most of the twenty other varsity runners to get ahead of him. Through the first mile, Eric confidently works his way forward. By the time they reach the course's big hill, he's right behind Rick. As they begin the climb, Rick starts to labor. Eric keeps his momentum and passes him. He presses on past a group of three--one from Hammond, one from Fitch, and Kyle, who looks over at him and stares. They pass a group of cheering

Regal fans at the top of the hill, but all Eric can hear is Paul, who's practically jumping out of his shoes.

As they top the rise and start down, Eric gains on a couple of Fitch runners. Just in front of them is Mike. They freewheel out onto the flat approach to the finish, about 300 meters away. The spectators are clapping as Vance crosses the finish in first place. Ten seconds later, two Hammond runners finish. With about 200 meters to run, Mike is exhausted and tightening up. The two Fitch runners catch him and start to pass. Mike looks over but makes no effort to hold them off. Eric has followed the Fitch runners into the finishing stretch and now swings wide and makes a big move, passing Mike and advances on the two Fitch boys. Mike gives a passive glance to the third runner going by and is surprised to see—it's Eric. Mike, terrified by the thought of losing to a freshman, breaks into a desperate sprint. One hundred meters from the finish, with Eric about a meter ahead, they both pass the two Fitch runners. With twenty-five meters to go, Eric glances back: Mike is gradually falling behind and the two Fitch runners are well back. Relieved, Eric relaxes slightly. Mike sees Eric ease up and produces a frantic final effort. Two steps from the finish, Eric is shocked to see Mike right beside him. He tries to respond, but Mike has the momentum and dives across the finish line half a second ahead. Mike lands full-length and skids to a stop on the hard-packed dirt as the crowd gasps. He curls onto his side, bleeding from ugly scrapes on his forearms and knees. Eric is still stunned by being passed, but he goes over to help.

"Are you all right?" Eric says carefully, trying to help Mike up.

"Get off me! Lemme go. I can get up," Mike snaps. "Just go on ahead." Eric, breathing hard and streaming sweat, hesitates.

"Go on!" Mike orders. Disheartened, Eric turns and walks through the finish chute. He is met at the end of the chute by Coach Morris.

"Eric, always run hard through the finish line," the coach says. "Don't slow down until after you cross it. Got it?"

"I got it."

"Never back off like that. You hear me?"

"Yes, sir."

Seemingly satisfied, the coach walks toward Mike, who looks embarrassed as he's helped up by several spectators.

"Thanks," Mike says, trying to steady himself. Eric glances at Mike and walks away, bewildered and upset.

"Keep moving," an official calls out. Mike limps through the chute as Coach Morris walks up to him.

"Hey, Coach."

"I wish you'd work that hard against opponents instead of competing with your teammates. You really disappoint me," Coach says and walks away.

After the last race, the team groups up at their encampment. Mike cleans debris from his scraped forearms. Rick struggles to open a bag of chips while Eric looks at Mike dabbing at his arms with a wad of bloody Kleenex. Rick pulls harder at the edges of the bag and it explodes, sending chips flying everywhere. They rain down on Eric and a few land on Mike, who is now wrapping white adhesive tape over a makeshift bandage. Maria sits close by with

Mr. Tate, waiting for news on the outcome of the race. The team notices Coach Morris walking toward them. They all watch him, trying to read his expression for a clue on the results. Coach Morris is stopped by the coach from Fitch High, who shakes his hand.

"Looks good," Mike says hopefully.

Coach Morris continues over to where the team sits on the grass.

"Well, team, this is a significant day. We didn't get third."

"You mean we didn't get last, like last year?" Mike interjects.

"That's right. Because you and Eric passed two Fitch runners at the end, we beat Fitch. We took second!"

The boys exchange shocked expressions that turn to smiles. Then Mike shouts out a long, wild "Yeeeaaaahhhh!!" The rest of the runners join in with whoops and cheers, high-fiving and pumping fists in the air.

"We finally broke our losing streak," Coach Morris goes on. "What timing—we're getting our pictures taken tomorrow. How about some smiles this time? And please wash your uniforms tonight, because that's what you'll be wearing. Let's not have a repeat of last year with the "authentic" muddy uniforms, okay?"

He walks off, writing on his clipboard.

The Regal high varsity boys' cross country team members are sitting on the school's bleachers. They're getting ready for their team picture. Coach Morris gets last-minute instructions from the photographer as the kids wait patiently. Eric and Paul are standing off to the side. Eric's tucking in his singlet. Coach Morris periodically looks up to check the boys.

"You better get in there, you're varsity now," Paul says. Eric excitedly moves into the group next to Mike, who looks over at him and then elbows him hard in the side. Eric grabs his side and turns to look at Mike.

"Not so fast," Mike says. "Running varsity was a one-shot deal. This is for the yearbook. Freshmen over there." He elbows Eric again, and Eric doubles over as he moves away from him. Mike points to where a startled Paul is standing toward the side of the group. Eric looks up to see Ellie crossing her arms and looking angrily at Mike, who's adjusting the bandages on his forearms.

"Mike, leave him alone. Let him sit," Ellie demands. Eric is too upset to even acknowledge Ellie defending him.

Barry looks at Rick and notices chocolate smears on his face but then notices something else. Rick is clutching a science book close to his side.

"What's that?" Barry asks.

"A book."

"I can *see* it's a *book*, but why do you have it with you?"

"To study."

Mike rolls his eyes. "You never study."

"I know, but if I'm holding a book in the picture it will make me look smart."

"Not with chocolate all over your mouth!" Taylor remarks. Rick touches his lips and then looks at his fingers. Then he wipes his mouth thoroughly with the back of his hand.

"Whoa. Good thing Coach isn't looking," Rick says.

Barry notices something dark on Rick's palm.

"Dude, you get a tattoo or something? What is that all over your hand?"

"Um, it's my notes. So I know what chapters to study for the test next week."

Kyle, Taylor, and Barry laugh. Rick joins in. "Why's that funny?" he asks. They ignore him.

Coach Morris returns from talking to the photographer and notices Eric walking toward Paul.

"Hey, Eric," he calls. "Get back where you belong!"

Confused, Eric returns to where he was originally standing distrustfully next to Mike.

"Coach, is this permanent? Eric's on varsity?" Mike asks.

"As permanent as the scars you'll have on your arms, Mike."

"He might *letter* in varsity," Paul adds.

"We'll see," Coach Morris says.

"No freshman has ever lettered varsity," Vance says seriously.

"There's a first time for everything," Paul replies.

"The team supplies the uniform, but you have to buy your letterman jacket," Barry tells Eric as he rejoins the group. "I'm on the three-year plan to score my varsity letter."

"Yeah, and you're on the five-year plan to graduate," Taylor adds. The group laughs.

Coach Morris takes his position beside the group. The team is in clean uniforms and ready for the photograph when the coach notices the book in Rick's hand.

"Rick, put the book down. Everybody smile."

Everyone smiles and looks at the camera except Rick, who stares down at his science book just as the flash goes off.

That evening, Eric is excited as he gets home from practice. He's had a good day: he ran well in practice, and he got to wear his varsity uniform in the school picture. Dale is sitting on the couch waiting for him. Eric senses something is wrong: his dad is never home this early and the look on his face is serious.

"Eric, I need to speak with you," Dale calls out.

Eric knows the tone and it's not good. He walks to the edge of the entryway and stops. He looks at his dad, confused.

"Your teacher Miss Anderson called today. She says you're failing her history class and Mr. Lopez's biology class."

Eric looks down, avoiding his father's eyes.

"Did you know about this?"

"Yes...kind of," Eric says, troubled. "I know I'm not doing well, but I didn't know I was *failing*."

Maria comes out from the hallway, looking curious.

"What's going on?" she asks. Eric keeps his eyes on the floor.

"Eric is failing in school," he tells her.

"What?"

"History and biology," Dale says.

"Eric, look at us. Is this true?" Maria asks.

"Sit down, son," his father demands. Eric sits facing his mom and dad in the living room, dread on his face.

"You have to understand something. You're in school to learn, if you fail your classes, you can't go to college. Why do you think I was pushing football? So that you can go to college, maybe get a scholarship the same way I did. My father couldn't afford to send me, either. I could only get that football scholarship because I did well with my grades. I don't make enough money to put you through college."

Maria listens with concern.

"Now, if running is interfering with your grades, you'll have to stop running. This is the same thing you did in middle school, with the video games. You weren't studying. When you stopped those games, you did really well. But you had to be disciplined. The same thing applies here."

Eric starts to say something, then stops.

"I'm giving you a chance to fix this before I step in," Dale goes on. "Understood? Now go to your room and study."

"Yes, sir," Eric says, discouraged. He walks slowly down the hallway to his room. Once Eric is out of earshot, Dale turns to Maria.

"I told you this running stuff was a bad idea," he tells her.

"Don't blame this on running. If anything, running gives you more discipline. It did for me."

"Well, it's not working for him," Dale insists. "In fact, it's taking all his time away from his homework."

"Look, he just doesn't know how to balance his time between sports and studying. You and I have been in sports and we passed our classes. Just give him another chance. I'll keep an eye on him."

"Okay, but if he fails one more test, he has to quit running."

Dale walks out of the room, leaving Maria with a worried look on her face.

The weather is overcast as Eric leaves the house. He steps into the chilly morning air and begins to jog. He reaches the city limit sign, runs underneath it, and starts his watch. With no invitational race this weekend, he starts fast to simulate a race. After a hundred meters he slows down and settles into pace. Eric feels good and in control running along the side of the road. From behind, he hears some yelling. He looks back to see a car he doesn't recognize with a couple of girls waving out the window.

"Whoop! Whoop!" they yell as they speed past.

Eric just smiles and waves. He arrives at the isolated intersection on Verdugo Road. He looks at his watch, which reads 17:58.

Eric yells, "Whoop! Whoop!" as he turns around to go back.

When he has about a half-mile left to run, Eric still feels good. He decides to try to sprint the last 300 meters to the finish. Just as he accelerates, Eric hears a car horn behind him. He looks back to see a car he *does* recognize, a red Volkswagen. It's Ellie and Vanetta.

"Go, Eric!" Ellie yells out, honking a few times. Ellie waves; Vanetta just glances over at Eric as they drive by. He's all smiles and waves back before they disappear up ahead around the corner. Eric keeps sprinting to the sign and stops his watch as he races under it. He checks his time as he slows to a jog. The watch reads 35:28.

That afternoon, Eric sits at his desk. His watch is on the desktop. Instead of turning on his computer, he reaches for his notebook. He opens it to the first page. Below a heading that reads:

EL PASEO ROAD COURSE

Eric has written the times he's recorded:

38:50

37:51

36:37

35:59

He happily writes "35:28" below the last record. He takes a moment to appreciate his improvement. He wonders if he's gaining on Todd Bryce, or if Bryce is training just as hard and also improving his times. Eric looks at his video-game controller and is tempted, but he turns his attention to his history book instead. He opens it and starts to read. There's a knock at the door.

"Come in," Eric says. Maria pokes her head into the room.

"How's the studying?"

"So far so good."

"Great," she says before quietly closing the door.

Eric knows that he has to buckle down or his running days are over. He wishes he could just do the things he's good at, like video games and running, but he knows that's not realistic. He's been through a lot so far—a new school, the struggle against the bullies, and trying to get along with teammates like Mike. He figures there's a lot he has to learn. He returns to the book and tries to forget about his concerns.

The lunchtime bell has rung, and Eric is out of class early. He looks up to see storm clouds darkening the sky as he walks toward his locker. Coach Morris intercepts him.

"Eric, I've been looking for you. To my office," he says, ushering a curious Eric off to his room.

They walk into the sparsely decorated office.

"Have a seat," Coach says in a stern tone. Eric starts to get a little nervous wondering what he's done. He hasn't snitched on Mike about the pool-playing, so he can't imagine what it's about, but knows he's in trouble.

"Eric, I got a call from Miss Anderson."

"She called you, too? She already called my parents!"

"Well, that's her job, to inform your parents and me. You know, all sports require the students participating to have a grade-point average of C or better."

"I know, my dad told me," Eric says, disconcerted.

"If you don't bring your grades up, I'm afraid you can't compete. Varsity *or* frosh-soph. Basically, you'll be off the team.

"No," Eric says, horrified.

"You can't continue until your grades improve and stay that way. You follow me?" He says.

"Yes, Coach," Eric replies.

"I've had to kick plenty of kids off the team. Doesn't matter how fast you are, there's no fooling around when it comes to school. Lots of athletes can't balance sports and their classes. I've watched you practice and improve over the season, but you have to understand something. The same amount of practice and commitment you've been putting into this team, you have to put into your studies. You can't neglect them. Now, I looked up your grades for middle school and they were fine. So, the problem seems to lie in how you're balancing the two. Is that right?"

"Yes, sir. I've been spending more time on running."

"Now, I can get a tutor for you if you need one, but I have to see improvement."

"No, I don't need a tutor, Coach," Eric says, determination in his voice. "I guess you're right. I haven't been putting enough effort into studying."

"Don't let your talent go to waste by not studying," Coach stresses before adding, "I'll see you at practice, but remember, as of now you're on trial. Until I see improvement."

"Yes, sir," Eric says. The coach escorts him out of his office.

Paul is anxiously looking around the campus. He sees Eric, with his head lowered, walking to his locker. Paul runs over.

"I've been looking all over for you! I thought we were having lunch together."

"I'm not hungry."

"What's wrong?" Paul asks.

"I'm failing history and biology. Miss Anderson called my parents and Coach. Now Coach tells me I'm off the team if my grades don't improve."

"Oh, man. I have to get all A's or my dad grounds me," Paul says.

"I've got all these distractions. Like, I'm always on the lookout for those jerks from the football team, Beef and Crush. I don't know if I should tell my parents. I don't want my dad to think I can't take care of myself. I just don't know what to do."

"Why don't you tell Coach?"

"I can't. He's already upset with me,"

"Maybe those dorks will get tired of chasing you."

"You think?"

"Not really, but there's always the possibility they'll switch targets," Paul says. "As long as they don't come after me again."

"Yeah," Eric says with a chuckle, remembering his first meeting with Paul.

Paul looks up at the overcast sky. He looks worried as he turns toward Eric.

"If you get kicked off the team, you can't run league finals."

"I know."

"Well, look, if you want, let's go to the library after practice and I'll help you."

Eric looks at Paul and feels a rush of gratitude, thinking about how complete his friend's support has been through the whole season. He holds out a hand.

"Thanks, Paul."

Paul grabs his hand and shakes it. "You got it."

They both look up as the clouds deliver the downpour that the sky had been threatening all morning. Together, they sprint toward the cafeteria.

Later, as the rainstorm continues, Mike chalks his cue in the community center and stares out a large, rain-spattered window. A few people dash past with umbrellas and newspapers held over their heads. At the pool table, Barry is waiting his turn while

Taylor and Rick watch. They notice Vance running past the window, his clothes soaked, hair plastered to his head.

"Running in the rain *sucks*!" Barry says. "I'm missing a lot of workouts. I wish we had an indoor track, like they do back East. How can we stay in shape?"

"What do you think this is, a prep school?" asks Mike. "You gotta be creative. Go downtown to the tallest building and run the stairs. Use the railings, and it will buff your arms up as well."

"Or you could work on a farm baling hay," Taylor suggests. "My cousin did that one summer. Said it was better than weights. Gets rid of those girly hands, too."

"Look who's talking," replies Rick. "Hey, I got a good one. Find an old lady with a steep yard and offer to mow her grass with a push mower. Mowing uphill is a bitch! That'll keep you in shape."

Barry threatens to hit Rick's groin, and Rick quickly moves away, nearer to the window.

"You dork!" Barry yells after him. "You can't cut grass in the rain!"

The boys laugh as Eric runs into view of the window.

"Speaking of dorks, look at the drowning rat!" Rick says.

They all get quiet as they watch Eric getting smaller, running away on the rain-soaked pathway.

Rick shakes his head. "You believe that freshman?! Thinks he's Vance Junior. If Vance ran blindfolded, he'd do it, too."

Mike points his cue at the window. "He tries to pass me again, he'll get an elbow to the head." Suddenly he tosses the cue onto the table. "Screw it," he says, and runs out the door.

The others look at one another. Through the window they see Rick take off down the path.

"No, no, no. No way," Barry says. "I'm not going to let him get an edge on me!" Barry says. "I'll see you two losers later." He puts down his cue and jogs toward the door just as a small figure in a full yellow rain suit runs past the window.

Taylor and Rick explode in laughter, pointing out the window. "Check out Paul!" Rick shouts.

"He's dressed for friggin' *Deadliest Catch*," Barry says, and then he sprints out into the driving rain.

Taylor and Rick laugh. Kyle and the girls' team appear at the window just before Barry rushes past. He runs right through a huge puddle and splashes the girls, who dodge out of his way as he dashes past, head down, wincing.

"Hey! Watch it!" The girls yell.

"What morons! Nothing's going to get me to go out there," Rick declares.

They turn back to the game and freeze. Through the side window, they see Coach Morris's van pull up outside.

"Well, *almost* nothing!" Rick yells. They drop their cues and sprint out the back door.

A few seconds later, Coach Morris walks briskly through the front door and into the game room. He looks at the pool table:

a game in progress but with no players. He notices the four cues on the table top. He sets his jaw and strides back out to his van.

The rain is still unyielding and is blasting nearly sideways in a whipping wind. Mike is running hard, trying to catch up to Eric. He looks up occasionally to see Eric through the blur. Soon he is frustrated to notice that Eric is actually getting further away. Mike gives up and begins to jog, watching Eric disappear into the distance.

Barry is straining, hard, too, fighting the wind. He squints to protect his eyes and sees that he's closing up rapidly on a runner ahead. He's surprised to see that it's Mike, jogging. Barry catches up in short order.

"Freshman dropped you, huh?" Barry asks.

"No!" Mike says angrily. "I'm just…I'm luring him into a false sense of security."

"So where are we going to cut the course?" Barry says slyly.

"How did you know what I was thinking?"

"Because that's what I would do if I couldn't catch him," Barry says matter-of-factly.

"You putz. Follow me," Mike says as he stomps in a puddle, trying to splash Barry. Still a step ahead, Barry avoids the spray of water. Behind them and catching up slowly are Taylor and Rick. They see Mike and Barry turn off course up ahead. Taylor and Rick look at each other and take the short cut, too.

Despite the monster downpour, Eric is running comfortably on the wet sidewalk, clicking off close to six-minute miles, oblivious to all the drama he has caused among his teammates. He's soaked, but his shoes and socks aren't too heavy because he's avoided the puddles. He thinks he can see someone running ahead of. Could it be Vance? Eric has never been able to even see him this close to the finish. Excited, Eric picks up the pace, still feeling fast despite the constant wind and pelting rain. He's gaining on the runner in front—and it's definitely Vance. Focusing completely on Vance's back, he's unaware of Mike and Barry emerging from behind a building on a side street. As he passes the corner, they take off after him. Eric's concentration is broken by a car horn honking from behind. Eric looks back and is surprised to see the approaching car passing Barry and Mike gaining on him. Eric is baffled. Did he make a wrong turn? How did Mike and Barry catch up? Eric picks up his speed to stay ahead and a race is on.

The pouring rain continues as the boys come in sight of the school. Barry drops just behind Mike; Eric has a ten-meter lead as they reach the last street-crossing. Eric slows to let a car cross. With all this distraction, he's lost sight of Vance. He glances back to see Mike and Barry still getting closer. Eric speeds up again, trying to hold his rhythm. Mike stays close, but Barry begins to drop back. Eric is nearly exhausted, breathing hard, struggling to maintain his speed as Mike closes in on him. Eric reaches the edge of campus first and slows to make the turn onto the slippery grass field, and Mike finally catches up. But Mike makes the turn too fast and goes wide, while Eric keeps his speed out of the turn and onto the rain-soaked field.

Eric glances back to see Mike straining to catch up. Eric races straight through the field, splashing through all the puddles in his path. After a few more feet, Eric looks back again to see his lead is growing. While he turns, his foot slides and slips from under him. He falls flat into a puddle, making a big splash. Mike's strained face shifts into a big smile as he passes Eric, practically stepping over him and waving good-bye while running to the finish.

Eric starts to stand, but when he puts weight on his right ankle, a shooting pain stops him. "Aw, crap," Eric says. He sits back down.

"Ha, ha," Barry says as he passes by, smiling and laughing, while Eric crawls to the side of the puddle.

The rain continues to fall. Eric prods his ankle, feeling for anything painful.

"Are you okay?" a female voice says above him. Eric is almost afraid to look up. It's Ellie, staring down at him. He wishes she wasn't there.

"Need help?" she asks.

"Yeah, I might have twisted my ankle. No big deal. I stepped on something," he says, starting to stand up on his left leg.

"Let me help you up," Ellie says, giving him a hand. He reluctantly takes it. He gets up and looks away from her.

"Do you think you can walk on it?" she asks.

"I don't know," he says, gingerly putting more weight on his right foot. The ankle feels sore but he can stand on it. "I think it's okay."

"I'll help you to the locker room," she says.

"It's okay, I can make it," Eric says. He wipes his face with his wet shirt, which doesn't help much.

"I wonder where Coach is?" she says as they start to walk. Eric's drenched shoes squish out water with each step. "I knew

something was up when I saw them take a short cut. You can't let those boys get to you."

"They took a short cut?"

"Look, just because you're on the team doesn't mean that they're going to be nice to you. You're still a freshman, and they're immature," Ellie says.

"*That's* how they caught up," Eric says, beginning to shiver as they reach the entrance to the locker rooms.

"You got them on the run," Ellie says.

"I guess so."

"I hope your ankle's okay," she says.

Eric opens the door and limps into the locker room. He's frustrated as he grabs a towel to wipe off his face. He hobbles to a bench, sits down, and stares at his ankle. It hurts, but how bad is it? What if he's injured again? What will he say to his dad? And Coach? How can he compete with Bryce now? Eric's thoughts are interrupted by the sounds of Mike and Barry laughing in the background. Eric gets up, then sits back down. He's cold but decides to wait for Mike and Barry to leave. Eric sits quietly alone, shivering, wet, and muddy.

Central Inland League Finals

It's a sunny day for the League finals at Lower Arrow Park. Teams from Fitch, Hammond, Newark, Rockford, and Wayland are ready to compete against Regal and one another. The Regal team is in good spirits as they jog up to Coach Morris near the starting line. Eric and Paul show up late to the start.

"Where have you been?" Coach asks Eric.

"The bathroom, Coach," Eric says. Coach notices that he's favoring his right foot.

"What's wrong with your foot?"

"I, uh, I aggravated my ankle injury," Eric remarks. The other runners look at him. Mike looks down with a hint of guilt on his face.

"Are you okay to run?" Coach asks.

"Yeah, Coach. I'm just being careful."

"Are you sure?"

Paul interrupts. "He's fine, Coach, and he's been icing his ankle."

"I didn't ask you," Coach shoots back.

"I'm fine, Coach, I can run," Eric says.

"Okay, but if I see you limping, I'll pull you out," Coach says. Coach looks around at his team, all wearing their new team sweats and tops except for Kyle.

"What do you guys think of the new sweats?" Coach Morris asks them.

Rick raises his hand. Barry sees an opportunity to hit Rick in the groin and does so.

Coach turns and gives them a stern look. "Hey. What's the matter with you guys? Stop screwing around. You got the uniform on. It's time to work. This is the end of the season." He looks at Barry. "For most of you it'll be your last race. Make it count."

He nods at Kyle, who's standing toward the back. "Where's your team top?"

"Over there," Kyle points toward the team camp in the distance.

"Go get it. We give you new sweats and you're wearing that?"

"I like my hoodie, Coach."

"Take it off! Now. Go on. We haven't got all day."

He scans the rest of the runners. "I want you guys to look like a team at least once this season. No more fooling around, no more nonsense."

Kyle returns after a few minutes with his new top on. The old top's hood sticks out from underneath and over the back collar of the new team top. His teammates notice the hood and laugh. Coach is not amused and gives Kyle an annoyed look.

"Get your sweats off," Coach Morris says. "We should be starting any minute. Warm up and stretch—now's the time to get loose."

"Run hard, but try to pace yourself," Coach says to Barry. "Just don't die."

"You know, I've never seen anyone really *die*," Rick whispers to Barry.

"It's not literal, dumbass," Barry answers.

An official walks past them. "One minute," he says.

Coach Morris looks over the group. "Sixty seconds, boys. Let's go!"

"Wait—is it sixty seconds or one minute?" Rick asks.

The team laughs.

"Okay. That's enough. Focus," Coach says.

The Regal team joins the other five teams at the starting line. The starter signals for everyone to take their positions. Vance and Eric take their places in front.

"Runners *set* …"

The gun sounds and the runners take off. Vance and Eric sprint ahead. Eric is relieved to find that his ankle isn't giving him trouble. Spectators, including Maria and Mr. Tate crowd close to a bridge as the runners disappear from view. After a few minutes they return, heading toward the bridge. Vance has a small lead as he crosses the bridge and turns onto the path along the canal. Close behind are two Hammond runners, followed by Eric, Taylor, and Mike. Two seconds farther back are five boys from the Rockford team. Next comes a mass of about twenty-five runners that includes Barry and Kyle. Ten seconds later, Rick crosses the bridge among the stragglers.

On the canal path, the crowd cheers as Vance runs past, widening his lead. Forty meters back, Eric runs with Hammond's top two men. Mike struggles to stay with them. Thirty yards farther back, the pack of Rockford men lead the large group, which has caught Taylor. Barry and Kyle are near the back of the group. Coach Morris and Paul watch in astonishment as Rick runs past them, third from last in the field of forty-two runners.

With 500 meters left, Vance has a huge lead. Eric is hanging with the Hammond duo as Mike falls back and is passed by one runner, then another in the disintegrating pack.

Vance crosses the finish line and jogs easily to a stop. He calmly pulls the label off his number and hands it to a waiting girl, then turns to watch the other runners finish. The two Hammond runners are sprinting side by side and gradually pulling ahead of Eric, who's fighting hard. Eric holds his sprint to the line and finishes fourth. A group of Rockford and Wayland runners battle down the stretch and stagger into one another in the finish chute; behind them, an anguished Mike crosses the line in eighth place, rips off his label, and throws it angrily in the direction of the stat girl, who tries to pick it up as Mike brushes past her and stomps through the chute. Behind him, runners from Newark and Rockford take ninth and tenth places. The rest of the field follows, first in a dense group, then in a thinning single file.

Just past the finish chute, Vance and Eric are joined by Coach Morris and Paul. Mike approaches, and Eric turns to congratulate him, then decides it isn't a good idea. Mike walks straight past the group.

"Mike," Coach Morris calls out. "If you want to run better, you should have spent less time playing pool."

Eric is surprised. Coach knows that Mike plays pool instead of running workouts? Mike turns back to look at Coach.

"What, you thought I didn't know?" Coach Morris says to him. "I know where you guys go," pointing a finger at Mike. "You do just enough to get by. You go through the motions. I'd like to see you run fast, but I can't make you do it. You have to motivate yourself. You just took eighth place in League! You have so much potential, but you're *wasting* it. It's your choice to be mediocre, but if I catch you playing pool again, I'll kick you off the team and save you any more embarrassment!"

Mike kicks at some grass in frustration as he walks away from the coach. Just then Barry storms past and follows Mike. Paul is counting under his breath, trying to figure out the team score.

"Regardless of what Barry thinks, we ran great today," Coach says. "Three in the top ten—that's amazing. Now we just have to see where Barry and Taylor placed. Kyle and Rick didn't help us much."

He eagerly heads for the officials' table and Paul follows. Vance gets interested and goes after them. Coach Morris takes a position behind the table to try to see the pages of results from the race, with Paul and Vance taking a position behind him.

Coach, Vance, and Paul peer over at the pages trying to read the ongoing results of the race in progress. After Vance in first, Eric in fourth, and Mike in eighth, they see Barry listed in seventeenth and Taylor in nineteenth.

"That's forty-nine!" Coach Morris says, astonishment on his face. "That's the best score we've ever had!"

"How do they get the score at league Finals?" Eric asks.

"Same as in a dual meet—first five team members to finish," Paul replies. "You add up their places. First is one point, second is two, and so on. Low score wins, like golf."

The announcer asks for the crowd's attention. "In the varsity boys' competition, we have our closest team race in Central Inland League history! The top three teams will be going to the California Interscholastic Federation Prelims. They are: In third place, with fifty-two points… Rockford High School!"

Rockford's team and fans cheer, more in relief than joy. Their season's not over.

"In second place…"

The Regal team stands in near-disbelief as they wait to hear the words.

"…with fifty points—Hammond High School!"

As the Hammond crowd dances and yells, Coach Morris and Vance look at each other quietly.

"Nice job, Coach," Vance says.

"And in first place, with an amazing performance, scoring forty-nine points, is our new league champion… Regal High School!"

The whole Regal team, even Barry and Mike, leap into the air and shout. Rick falls backward on the grass and lands spread-eagled in shock. The girls' team members hug the boys, the boys lift them up off their feet, and the parents stand around shaking their heads in happy bewilderment. The Hammond and Rockford coaches come over and shake Coach Morris's hand. Their varsity teams follow and congratulate the Regal boys.

Coach Morris reaches for a bag and pulls out red, yellow, and pink shirts.

"And the honors just keep on coming," he says.

He flings red **<17** shirts to Taylor and Barry, then a yellow **<16** to Eric, who proudly opens it up. He tosses a pink shirt to Grace. Grace eagerly unfurls the shirt to reveal **<18** and screams with delight. Ellie and Katy congratulate her.

"Just one more shirt," announces Coach Morris. Everyone grows quiet. Eric sees Coach looking at Paul, who's oblivious, and starts a slow, steady clap. Paul looks at him and does a double-take as Coach tosses him a pink **<18** shirt. He glances around at his teammates, who are all clapping now, and starts to smile—but then he looks at the pink shirt again.

"Paul, a sub-eighteen is a sub-eighteen," says Coach Morris.

"Coach, a pink shirt is a pink shirt!" Paul says. "Don't you have another color?"

"Yes, we do, Paul," Coach says. "You'll get that one when you run a minute faster."

That evening, Eric and Paul are in front of the computer in Paul's room, reading a message-board thread about high school cross country.

"They're talking about us," Paul says.

"Yeah."

"Check out this headline," Paul says. "'The pigs are flying! Regal won the league championship.' Then someone called

'MVAL' says, 'What a fluke. Hammond wasn't at full strength. Wait 'til next week at prelims.'"

"Who or what is 'MVAL'?" Eric asks.

"I don't know—I'm sure it's code for something."

"And then someone called 'Mowry' says, 'Vance is a stud,'" Eric reads.

"Must be a girl," Paul mutters.

Eric continues to read. "'And they have that fast freshman who came out of nowhere.'"

"Hey, that's you, Eric," Paul says. "Some guy named 'Spike' says, 'That kid is one to watch.'"

"Wow… look at this screen name," Eric says. "'Distance Freak.' He says, 'The one to watch is Todd Bryce. He's won every freshman race there is. Now he runs varsity. He was sixth at Mount SAC.'"

"Then 'Cross Country Dude' says, 'Bryce won the Griffith Invite and beat that Regal freshman,'" Paul reads. "Then someone called 'Spike' says, 'That was early in the season. The Regal kid keeps getting faster.'"

"Look at what this 'Waffle Racer' guy says: 'Bryce is the fastest kid on the whole Skyline team.'"

"Yeah," says Paul, "but Skyline doesn't have a Vance on the team."

"That's right," Eric says. "Too bad for them."

As Eric reaches school the next day, he glances out of habit at the digital ground sign. He does a double take.

REGAL X-COUNTRY

Varsity Boys League Champs!!

Congratz: Vance, Taylor, Kyle, Barry, Mike, Rick,

and Eric

Eric is impressed that the whole varsity team is named. No football announcement in sight—it's all about cross country. Eric turns around to see if other students are noticing the monumental event. The kids walking by don't give the sign more than a passing glance—except one, who has stopped in front of it. It's Paul. He notices Eric and runs over to share the moment.

"This is great. We put cross country on the map. Everyone knows your names!" Paul says as they both admire the sign. They tap knuckles together before walking on to their lockers.

Vance, Taylor, and Barry meet in the middle of campus wearing their cross country team sweats. They congratulate one another. Nearby, the school's varsity quarterback, Russell Burke, is talking with two linemen. They're all are seniors wearing their football jerseys. When Russell sees the cross country boys, he makes his way over to where they're standing. The linemen follow.

"Hey, you guys see the misprint in today's sports page? It says our cross country team won the League Championship."

"Ain't no misprint, Russell," says Vance. "Take a look at the school sign out front. It says 'League Champs.' It's the real deal."

"That's a fact, Jack," adds Barry smiling broadly.

"Yup. And I was integral in the making of this landmark event," Taylor says.

Russell smiles. "Hey, congrats. So now you guys break out with the team gear."

"Yeah, well, we never won a meet before this year," Barry says.

"And not just a meet—we won the League Meet!" adds Taylor. "Our whole team's names are on that sign!" He slaps Barry a high-five.

"We knew we were getting better, but we didn't expect to win," says Vance. "This is an all-time high point for Regal cross country."

Russell chuckles. "Yeah, I don't know how you did it with baggage like these guys," He says to Vance.

Barry elbows Taylor. "See what happens? People get jealous when you accomplish something before they do."

"Yeah," agrees Taylor. "Can you say 'champions,' dude?"

"It's not too late to join our team," adds Vance, grinning at the linemen and Russell.

"No way," Russell replies. "The only time I run is when I see defensive linemen."

One of the linemen speaks up. "Or because the coach is punishing you."

Russell elbows him hard in the side and the lineman shuts up. Across campus the boys notice Ellie walking.

"I'd run after *her*," Russell says. "You guys are lucky. You get to hang out with her every day."

Ellie walks past and finds Eric sitting alone on a bench near the locker room entrance.

"That's the freshman that tried out for football," Russell remarks.

"His name's Eric Hunt. He's the number-two man on varsity," Vance says.

"He gets around for a freshman," Russell says.

"That's why his name is last on the announcement board," Taylor says.

Over on the bench, Ellie notices Eric's low spirits.

"What's wrong?" Ellie asks.

"I feel bad about beating the seniors," Eric says.

"So, you've bruised a few egos. They'll get over it," Ellie tells him. Ellie lets the words sink in for a few seconds.

"How's the ankle?" she adds.

"It's healing," he says sheepishly. Then, mustering some courage, he goes on. "Can I ask you something?"

"Sure."

"Except for Paul, most of the team doesn't even speak to me. Why do you talk to me?"

Ellie looks over at Eric and smiles to comfort him.

"Because I can relate. I've been there. I was a freshman when I joined the cheerleading squad. The other girls wouldn't talk to me, wouldn't let me in their clique. I was always alone," Ellie says.

"You?"

"So you know what I did?"

"What?"

"I trained. I started practicing every day, doing my moves, stretching. Even going to a gym, that's the way I got good. They couldn't ignore me after that," Ellie says, looking at Eric. "Sort of like what you're doing. Now I run to keep in shape."

"Wow…and now everyone wants to talk to you. You turned it completely around. You think I could do that?"

Ellie looks at him seriously, "When you work hard and get good at something, people notice it. Sooner or later, they respect you."

"You know, that's why I respect Vance," Eric says. "He's so determined. I'm just chasing him, hanging on as long as possible. Each race, I'm getting a little closer to him."

"Maybe soon, he'll be chasing you."

Eric laughs and leans back against the bench. Vanetta walks toward them and sees Ellie.

"Come on, Ellie, we got cheerleading practice," she calls out.

"Gotta go," Ellie says. She starts after Vannetta, then turns back to Eric. "See you at practice. Bye."

As she and Vanetta walk away, Eric can't take his eyes off Ellie. *She really believes in me,* he thinks. He's going over their conversation in his mind when Beef slams down next to him, putting his arm around him to keep him from getting up. Crush plops down on the other side, locking Eric in.

"Gotcha!" Beef says. "Don't look so surprised, Shrimp. I told you this day was coming, and now you're going to get it."

"You sure are," says Crush.

"How about we go to my office for a little chit-chat," Beef says. He reaches behind Eric's back, grabs his underwear, and pulls him up.

"Let's go," Beef says, pulling hard.

"Hey! Oww!" Eric yells.

"What? That hurt? I'm not even really pulling," Beef says.

"Ha! Ha! Ha! What a wimp," Crush says. He jumps up, lifts his hands high, and slaps them down on Eric's shoulders. "This way."

"Oww!" Eric yells again as he's pulled toward the locker room's double doors.

"That's more like it. That was *supposed* to hurt," Crush says with a laugh as they get to the doors.

"Your running days are over," Beef says.

"Yeah. You ever had a knee injury?" Crush adds. He lets go of Eric briefly to open one of the doors. Eric tries to break away, but Beef has a firm grip on his collar and shorts. Beef and Crush laugh as the door is opened.

"That's it? That's all you got? Ha! You're *dead*," Beef says, shoving Eric inside and against the wall while Crush closes the door behind them. The locker room is semi-dark, with a few lights on. Eric struggles in vain to break out of their grip.

"I'll bet you thought we'd never catch you," Crush crows.

"You shouldn't have run. It coulda been over nice and fast. Just hurt a *little*," Beef says menacingly.

"Yeah, but now it's gonna hurt a *lot*, and you'll have a permanent limp to remember us by," Crush says, shaking his fist in Eric's face. Just then, the locker doors swing open, throwing a shaft of daylight on Beef and Crush. They whip around to see Vance, Barry, and Taylor.

"What do you think you're doing? Let him go," Vance yells.

Beef grins. "Just straightening some things out with my buddy here. So get lost."

"Yeah, butt out. It's none of your business," Crush adds.

Vance walks closer to Beef, recognizing him from the football-throwing incident. He lowers his fists down his sides for a less threatening stance. "I said, *let him go*."

"No," Beef replies. "Whatcha gonna *do* about it, scrawny dude?"

"He ain't gonna do nothin'," Crush mocks.

"What could he do? He's just skin and bones," Beef says tauntingly.

"Ha! That's right. All these guys are wimps!" Crush crows.

"Well, first we'll call campus security. They'll be reporting what we've seen to the principal and the football coach. Four witnesses should be pretty convincing. Your parents will be interested, too, when the school contacts them," Vance says.

Beef and Crush show some concern before getting furious. "You don't want to snitch on us," Beef warns.

"That would be a *big* mistake," Crush adds.

"Your last mistake," Beef says threateningly.

"Yeah. You don't want us coming after you. Get it?" Crush asserts.

Suddenly the door swings open again and Russell walks in with the two linemen. Beef's and Crush's arrogance withers away. They shoot worried looks at each other.

"Hey Vance, maybe I can help. I speak football jargon," Russell says.

"Be my guest," Vance says stepping away.

Russell tilts his head, motioning to the linemen. They walk over and put their arms around Beef's and Crush's necks, their grip slowly tightening.

"Hey, Russell! What's going on?" Beef asks in a high-pitched voice.

"Yeah, how's it goin', Russell?" Crush asks.

"Let him go, Beef," Russell says.

Beef immediately loosens his hold on Eric.

"Now tell him you're sorry," Russell says to Beef.

"No. I'm not gonna say I'm sorry to that little twerp," Beef says.

"Oh, you're not?" Russell says. He moves in close, grabs Beef by his thick neck, and forces him down to his knees. One of the linemen grabs Beef's hand and bends his fingers back.

Beef screams.

"Now you're gonna apologize nicely. With feeling," Russell says. "Or do you want some more?" He glances at the lineman.

"No! No, wait—okay! Okay! I'm sorry!" Beef yells.

"I said with *feeling*," Russell says. He gives the lineman the go-ahead.

Beef starts to cry. "I'm *really, really* sorry," he sobs. Russell nods at the lineman and he releases Beef, who stumbles forward against a bench and starts wiping the tears from his eyes with his good hand. Russell turns his attention to Crush.

"Crush," Russell prods. "You too."

"I'm s-s-sorry! I'm really sorry!" Crush stutters, shaking all over. "Please don't hurt my hand! It was *his* idea—I d-d-didn't wanna hurt the kid—"

"You know what the penalty is for hazing a varsity athlete?" Russell asks.

Beef looks up in shock. "*Him*? He's *varsity*?"

"Don't you read the school announcements out front? His name's on it. These guys are league champions."

A dumbfounded Beef says, "That wimp?"

Russell rests his arm across Beef's back menacingly. "Pay attention. You need to learn a little respect for varsity athletes. You're lucky to be junior varsity. What *is* that penalty, guys? Was that the super-hot balm on a stick to warm their ass?"

"Then fit 'em for a trash can, right?" a lineman asks.

Eric interrupts. "Can we talk privately?" he asks Russell.

Russell nods. "Take them over there for a minute," he tells the linemen. Beef and Crush try their best to get away as they are escorted to a far corner of the locker room. Russell walks up to Eric. "What do you have in mind?"

Eric answers softly. "You know they've been chasing me and trying to mess me up all semester, but I think there's a better way to teach them a lesson. Maybe it should be more… educational." Eric smiles, and Russell gets it.

Russell smiles back. "Okay, we'll do it on the field, during practice, like what they did to you." Then he yells out, "Bring them over."

The two linemen bring Beef and Crush back to proceed with their disciplining. Russell steps in front of the bullies. "This kid just saved you morons from a half-hour of pure suffering," he says.

Beef and Crush manage timid idiotic smiles.

"Now get out of here."

Beef and Crush nod quickly and rush off. They bump and crash into lockers in their haste to get outside.

Russell nods to Eric. "Come watch practice. Front-row seat in the bleachers."

"See you there," Eric says. Russell smiles and walks out with the linemen. Eric turns to his teammates.

"Thanks, guys. They've been bullying me all season," Eric says.

"Not anymore," Vance says, opening the door for him. Once outside, Eric turns to Vance and the others and notices that they're all wearing the team sweat tops.

"You can wear those for school?" Eric asks.

"C'mon. We're league champs," Barry replies. He fakes a move to hit Eric in the groin and stops short. "Gotcha," he says.

"Let's go. We're gonna be late for class," Vance says.

Eric and the guys jog off together.

Behind the school that afternoon, Coach Morris addresses the boys' cross country team.

"Today is a time trial. We're going to see who's improving and who's not. We're running the three-mile course around the campus."

"Flat and fast," Paul says to Eric.

"Don't race all-out—just ninety percent of a race effort. I'm going to give you extra time to warm up. I want to see a good hard effort and really push the last half mile."

At the end of the time trial, Vance races across the grass field toward Coach Morris, who stands at the finish line holding a stopwatch. Vance finishes, then turns around to watch the rest of the team. Eric finishes next turns and watches, as Mike, Taylor, and Barry follow. Coach Morris reads out their times as they pass the finish line.

Coach Morris keeps the watch going, as Paul appears last, running hard. He flies around the final corner from a sidewalk through a gate to the field, then sprints toward the group. With fifty meters to go, he glances at his wrist. He lifts his knees higher, pumps his arms wildly, and crosses the line, his eyes squeezed shut. Coach Morris clicks the watch, and everyone looks at him as Paul staggers around in a little circle trying to catch his breath.

"Sixteen fifty-eight!" Coach says.

The team swarms around Paul to congratulate him. Coach Morris walks over and hands him a red T-shirt. Paul grabs it, gasps "Yes!" hugs it to his chest, then puts it on. Across the front in large black characters is **<17**. Mike and Rick thrust their fists in the air, and the rest of the team joins in.

As they walk toward the locker room, Eric puts his arm around Paul's shoulders.

"Ninety-percent effort, right?" he asks.

Paul smiles.

Twenty minutes later, Eric and Paul are sitting in the bleachers at football practice. They're munching on popcorn as if they're watching a good horror movie. On the field, a scrimmage is being played. Russell huddles with his team. Beef and Crush are on the opposing Junior varsity squad.

After the ball is hiked, Russell sprints left, drawing everyone's attention as he tries to find an open receiver. Meanwhile, on the right side of the field, two offensive linemen run straight for Beef and Crush and level them with fierce full-body blocks.

"Ouch! That must've hurt," Eric says.

A few plays later, when Beef and Crush have started to relax again, Russell directs a play their way. Both running backs veer off and run straight into Beef, while the fullback mows Crush down. The thumps are audible as they hit the ground hard.

In the stands, Eric says, "Ooooh!" Paul throws some popcorn into his mouth and says, "That looked painful."

At the end of the scrimmage, the coaches dismiss the players to run their required four laps. As the players break into a jog, the coaches walk off toward their office.

"I think that's it." Eric says. Paul smiles and nods as he chews a mouthful of popcorn..

Beef and Crush are jogging at the back of the group on the far side of the track. Noticing that the coaches are gone, they begin to cut across the infield to leave. Russell is ready and throws a football directly to each of them. Reluctantly they catch the balls—and then are horrified to see the whole varsity front line rushing directly at them. They glance at each other and toss the footballs away. It doesn't help: Beef and Crush are tackled, and more players pile on top of them.

Eric and Paul wince in unison.

"Whoa!" Eric says.

"Ouch!" Paul says. "Aren't you glad you're on the cross country team?"

"Sure am—football's too violent," Eric says, watching the players slowly rise from the dogpile. Russell looks over and gives Eric a thumbs-up. Eric gives him one back.

Mount SAC (California Southern Section Preliminaries)

The cross country course is crowded with teams getting ready to race. Vance leads the Regal team's warmup. They finish their jog and return to their encampment, which is marked by a school banner. Everyone grabs their duffel bags and takes out their racing shoes. Rick is frantically tossing things out of his bag.

"What's wrong?" Mike asks. "Looking for a candy bar?"

"No—I forgot my racing shoes!"

"Next time write it on your hand. Like you do for your homework," Barry tells him. "Run in your trainers."

"It doesn't matter anyway. We could run in ankle weights and qualify for the finals next week," Mike says.

Eric overhears the conversation as he double-knots his shoelaces. He nudges Paul, who's standing next to him.

"Hey, Paul, this race today—does it mean we don't have to win?"

"Just qualify. Put in a good effort but save yourself for next week."

"Yeah," Taylor agrees. "It's just a formality. As long as you're in the top fifty percent, it's a lock for us league champs."

"That means finish in the top half," Mike says proudly.

Coach Morris tells everyone it's time to go.

"Okay, team. We're at the prelims. We need to qualify for the finals. That means no slacking off. We've gone this far. You can keep your season alive," Coach says as they walk to the starting line.

"The top eight teams advance. I want you to work as a team. Run together. Push and pull each other along. Don't kill yourselves early. Let Vance run his own race. He knows what he's got to do. After halfway, I want you to push," Coach points at Mike. "Be a team out there. I don't want to see what happened last time. Use the downhills—let gravity work for you. Relax and roll. Now go qualify for the finals."

Rick looks down at his shoes. "You want me to run fast, put a fire under my feet."

The team peels off their sweats and hands them to Paul, who's standing on the sideline. The boys nod to one another and huddle up. Barry starts to hit Rick in the crotch but stops short, smiling.

"C'mon. Let's get serious now," Coach says.

Barry holds out his hand to Rick and they bump fists. Vance notices and stretches out his arm holding out his fist.

"Let's do this," Vance says, looking at the other guys.

The team follows his lead, crowding around in a circle, holding out their fists. The fists all cluster together and Eric bumps his fist with the team.

"Now what should we do?" Barry asks.

Vance tightens his fist to white knuckles. "Time to race."

"Do you feel the power?" Rick says.

"It's now or never," calls Mike.

Vance nods. "It's cross country time! Hands in," and they all put their hands together in the center of their circle.

"Rock this race. On three," Vance says. "One. Two. Three."

"*Rock! This! Race!*" they yell in unison. Then they bounce up and down on their toes and break into a jog toward their place on the starting line.

Eric feels very proud to be part of this team. There are more than one hundred competitors crowded on the airstrip. The Regal boys are all poised in position on the line, ready to run. Only two runners from each school are allowed on the front line. Vance and Taylor are on the line, with Mike and Eric behind them. Barry and Kyle are next followed by Rick at the end. The starter signals for them to take their places and get set. He raises his pistol. The Regal team goes from enthusiastic shouts to concentrated silence as they listen to the starter's commands.

"Runners *set!*"

The gun fires, and there is an immediate barrage of elbows. Eric almost runs into Mike, and to avoid bumping him, he slows slightly. The converging mass of runners press in from the sides and slow him further, and runners behind him are now pushing him forward down the airstrip. The runners reach the end of the strip and flood onto the hard-packed dirt trail. Suddenly a runner on Eric's left jumps directly into his path, and his knee crashes into Eric's left leg.

Eric fights to keep his balance but is pushed forward by other runners behind him. His right foot hits another runner's heel and suddenly he finds himself flat on his stomach in a cloud of dust, with other runners' shoes hitting the ground all around him. Another stumbling runner kicks the side of his head.

The spectators standing along the course are pointing at him as he slowly gets up, dazed and wincing. Coach Morris, looking worried, runs toward Eric along the fence lining the course. Eric catches a glimpse of the pack of competitors racing away down the valley loop. He starts brushing dirt off himself. He's fairly unscathed except for a scraped knee. He begins to limp off the course.

Coach Morris looks worried, as he watches Eric, while standing alongside the fence lining the course. He waves his arms to get Eric's attention.

"Eric, get going!" he yells. "Make it to the finish. We need your sticker! Run!"

Eric looks down at the label pinned to his singlet.

"Now!" Coach Morris yells.

Eric snaps out of his daze and quickly turns back to the course. The crowd cheers as he starts jogging. His right side and his head are aching from the fall, but he jogs through the pain and is slowly accelerating as he gets to the first turn. A roar goes up on the other side of the loop, and Eric glances over to see the leaders appear: Vance is in front, already three quarters of the way through the first loop.

Eric shakes off the stiffness and slowly picks up speed. He runs the two loops alone, and when he reaches the mile marker the rear pack of runners is within range. Going up the steep switchbacks, Eric begins to thread through a straggling line of slower runners.

Vance is in command as he powers up Poop-Out Hill with a large pack trailing about fifteen meters behind. In the pack,

around twentieth place, Mike leads Taylor, Barry, and Kyle. Rick has lost contact with his teammates. Eric, who has stretched out to full stride on the long downhill from the Switchbacks, reaches the hill about midway through the big field, still moving up.

Vance extends his lead on the flat stretch of trail behind Reservoir Hill. As he hits the hill, he has an eighty-yard lead and a certain victory. Meanwhile, Mike and Taylor hold their positions near twentieth place, followed closely by Barry.

Eric really picks up the pace on the flat, swerving through competitors, showing no signs of his fall except his dirt-streaked singlet. On Reservoir Hill, he continues to move through the middle of the pack. Halfway up the hill, he passes Rick. At the crest, he passes Kyle. Going down the hill he can only hold his position; he's up among the better runners now, and they're hard to pass. Kyle briefly tries to stay with Eric but soon gives up the attempt.

Eric continues to push hard. He's back on the airstrip, running on a straight line, and he passes two more runners. He can see Barry about thirty meters ahead. Near-sprinting, he makes the final right turn into the finish gauntlet.

Barry looks back to see Eric running hard, his head rolling from side to side, closing fast. Knowing that Eric won't catch him, Barry slows up over the last second upgrade before the finish, and on the last 15 level meters of terrain waits for Eric, looking back and giving him a nod of respect. Surprised, Eric crosses the finish line right alongside Barry.

Vance has won the race easily. Mike has finished next, in the teens, and Taylor has taken 20th place. Eric and Barry are 28th and 29th, the final scorers. Coach Morris, with Paul alongside, rushes over to congratulate the Regal runners. Eric looks toward

Coach Morris amid the flurry of hugs and handshakes. Coach Morris returns his smile with a thumbs-up.

"Eric, I need to talk to you," Coach says.

"Because I fell?" Eric says, knowing he's in for a pep talk.

"No, because you gave the other hundred and six guys a head start. Listen to me: whenever you fall down, get back up right away so you don't lose any more time," Coach says. "Don't stop, and never give up, understand? On this team, there's no room for error. You can't expect someone to pick up the slack if you drop out. You're it. As long as you're eligible, you run like it's all up to you to make sure the team qualifies."

"Yes, Coach," Eric replies.

After a cool-down jog in their sweats, the teams wait for the official results. The mood among the Regal boys is somber.

"I didn't think I really cared about it before, but now I'm stressing out," Kyle says.

"Whatever happens, it was a good season. I'm excited for next year," Katy says.

Rick starts to eat some chips. He pauses as Coach Morris walks toward them.

"Don't keep us in suspense," Mike pleads.

The coach plucks the bag out of Rick's hand. "Stop eating that junk," he says, and then eats a few chips. He looks at the ground. "Well," he says, "it was close."

"No! You mean we're the first league champions not to advance?" Rick asks.

"From making history to being history," Kyle says.

"Man!" Mike says, kicking the ground. "How many points back were we?"

"We were very close," Coach Morris says. He pauses, taking in all the sad faces before him. "But we shouldn't have been. Our qualifying should be undisputed!"

"You mean we made it?" asks Mike.

"We made it—but it shouldn't have been so close," Coach Morris says, looking at Eric. Eric looks down, embarrassed, as the team rejoices.

Eric and Paul excitedly run up to Coach Morris's office door. Eric is clutching two sheets of paper. They both knock on the door.

"Come in," Coach Morris says from inside. Paul opens the door and Eric runs in first proudly holding out the separate pages for Coach to see. In Eric's left hand is a graded biology test with a large "B+" circled at the top in red ink. In his right hand is a graded history test with a large red "B" on it.

Eric and Paul anxiously wait for Coach to read the grades. Coach looks up, smiles, and nods his approval. "Good. Now keep it up," he says. "Don't ever let your grades slip again."

"Okay," Eric says.

As the boys leave, Coach Morris hides his feelings. He knows Eric has put a lot of work and effort into running. Now he's gotten his grades up, too—because of the team. Coach Morris doesn't have the heart to tell him or the other team members the truth: that this is the last season for cross country at the school.

It is late afternoon at Regal High. The football players have disappeared, and the field is nearly deserted except for the cheerleading team. Eric enters the Regal campus and jogs onto the field at the end of his run. He notices Coach Morris standing just outside the locker room. Coach waves to Eric signaling practice is over and then disappears into the locker room. Eric jogs across the field, feeling good. He runs past the cheerleaders. Unbeknownst to Eric, they've got a cheer planned for him. Ellie waves at Eric to get his attention. He glances around to make sure it's him she's waving at. The cheerleaders all giggle and call out.

"Yes, you! Eric!"

They line up, pom-poms in their hands, and chant:

"Watch out! / He's here! / The course is clear!

'Cause you won't be near! / Victory is here!

Go-o-o-o, *Eric!!*"

Eric blushes and bashfully looks around to see if anyone is watching, then sheepishly waves as he jogs into the locker room.

Eric rushes home and runs directly into the kitchen, where Maria is preparing dinner.

"Hey, Mom," Eric says, stopping in front of the refrigerator.

"Hi," she says, watching him picking at a few loose fruit-shaped fridge magnets. He zips open his backpack and pulls out the two graded tests. He places the pages on the front of the refrigerator at his parents' eye level.

"What's this?" His mom asks, as Eric carefully places the magnets near the edges of the pages. She reads the grades.

"Oh, Eric—I'm so proud of you," she says, hugging him.

"Wait 'til Dad sees this!"

"I'll make sure he does."

When Dale comes home from work that evening, Eric is in the living room waiting for him. His dad hangs up his jacket and notices Eric anxiously sitting on the couch.

"Hi, Dad," Eric says, smiling at him.

"Hi," he says, looking curiously at him and stops, "Don't you have homework to do?"

"Yes, but Mom needs you in the kitchen first," Eric remarks.

"Okay—is everything all right?

"She has something to show you."

Puzzled, Dale walks into the kitchen. Eric jumps up from the couch and hides outside the kitchen doorway to see his dad's reaction to the grades. In the kitchen, Dale walks up to Marie, his back to the refrigerator, and looks curiously at her. She smiles at him.

"Why's everyone acting so strange around here?" he asks.

She playfully maneuvers him around into position. With her back to the refrigerator, she kisses her confused husband and steps aside to reveal the corrected tests. Finally catching on, he sees the grades. He senses Eric's presence and turns to see him in the doorway.

"Okay," he says. "But this doesn't mean you can stop studying."

"I know."

"Maybe the next one can be an A. You've gotten A's before."

A cheerful Eric walks into his room and sits at his computer desk. He picks up the video game controller and sets it down in front of him. Tempted to play, he traces the cord to the computer and disconnects it. He wraps the cord around the controller and places it carefully aside. He moves his biology book to the center of the desk, sighs, and opens it. He feels a sense of relief, as if a weight has been lifted, but he knows that there's a long road ahead.

Mount SAC (California Southern Section Finals)

Early Saturday morning the cross country team is in the van at the front of the school.

"All right let's settle down," Coach says.

"Hey, Coach. We put cross country on the map!" Mike announces.

"Can you believe it? The school wishes us luck," Barry quips getting a few laughs.

"I never thought I would see the day cross country would have something to announce," Taylor says.

"Okay. Let's make the school proud," Coach says, starting up the van. Eric and Paul look at each other with enthusiasm as the van engine starts up. The van pulls out away from the school digital ground sign. The sign headline reads:

CROSS COUNTRY

Good luck at Southern Section finals!

Following the school van are a few cars. Eric's mom and Paul's dad are two of the vehicles following them. Other vehicles also have parents from the team.

At Mount SAC, a Porta-John door swings open and Eric emerges to see a long line of runners waiting. He runs over to his team, all in their matching sweats. Kyle's hood sticks up over his collar as the team jogs.

Near the start line, the Royal boys peel off their sweats to race. Paul, who's there to watch and help out, has come prepared with a large laundry bag. He waits on the sideline as the team members toss their sweats at him.

"Hey! In the bag, guys!" Paul yells as the sweats land on top of him. Mike walks over to throw his sweats at Paul and notices the watch on his wrist. He grabs Paul's wrist to get a closer look at it.

"I'll put my sweats in the bag if you let me borrow your watch for the race," Mike says.

"What? Why?" Paul asks, pulling his wrist away from Mike and dropping some sweats.

"Lemme borrow it," Mike insists.

"How about you lemme borrow your letterman jacket?" Paul says.

"It wouldn't fit you, squirt," Mike says, still trying to get the watch.

Mike rolls his eyes at Paul, who relaxes his arm. "Okay, okay," he says, as he takes off his watch and hands it to Mike, who shoves the sweats into Paul's hands before joining the others, as they walk toward the starting line.

"I want Eric behind Vance," Coach says. Eric is a little surprised.

"Hey, Coach. That's my spot," Mike exclaims.

"Was your spot," Coach says.

"Well, he better start out fast."

"He will," Coach says, looking at Eric, who nods. "Stay together when you check in. Now, get going."

Just before lining up, the boys gather in a circle and shove their fists together in the center. Eric quietly revels in the solidarity.

"Don't be weak," chants Vance.

"Do you feel the power?" shouts Rick.

"Get on up!" Mike yells.

Vance grins at his teammates. "It's time for some Regal Cross Country!"

Vance wiggles his fingers and thrusts his hand skyward, prompting everyone to do the same.

"Yeah!" The team shouts in unison.

Under a large banner that reads CALIFORNIA SOUTHERN SECTION FINALS – START, one hundred and twenty-one anxious runners line up. Each team is single-file, with Regal near the middle. With a minute to go, final adjustments are made to shoes and numbered bibs. Some runners jog in place. Behind Vance, Eric stares at the ground, deep in thought, while others shift their weight from foot to foot. *Don't be nervous, Eric thinks. It's just another race. I know the course. Remember what Coach said: get out fast, stay focused and pace yourself.* Vance turns and nudges him.

"Hey, you okay?" Vance asks.

"Yeah, just a little nervous."

"Don't worry, once that gun goes off you'll forget all that," Vance says. "Just remember, stay behind me. Stick close to me," he adds. Eric looks up quickly. *Close to him?*

"Okay, I will," Eric replies, forgetting all about his fear.

"Relax and roll…relax and roll…," Barry repeats to himself behind Eric.

Taylor nudges Barry. "Look at me. Look right into my eyes. I'm going to hypnotize you. You're a horse. A friggin' thoroughbred. So don't think, just run."

Mike chuckles. "He's got the not-thinking part covered."

The boys all laugh except for Eric, who is focused on Vance.

The boys put on their game faces. The starter looks at the runners and waits for them to get settled. Once settled, the starter raises the starting pistol.

"Runners set…," the starter announces.

Some spectators are startled when the gun fires. Vance bolts, as does Eric, as all the runners take off down the straightaway. Because they're near the front, Eric is able to move to Vance's side. Most of the jockeying is going on right behind them. At the first turn, Eric lets Vance go ahead of him. Two Hammond runners cut in front of Eric. These three are the individual favorites, and they're already at the front. Rick dodges past Eric and reaches the front as well. Eric is a little nervous being out so fast, so close to Vance. He eases up and falls back a little. Taylor, Mike, and Barry have started out well and are near the front. After a quick first valley loop, the pace settles down at about the half-mile mark. The middle of the pack moves up, compelling Eric to stay closer to the leaders as the mob bunches up behind him. Eric's eyes are still fixed on Vance. During the second valley loop, Rick passes Vance, which puts him in the lead. The leaders are well under five minutes for the first mile.

They hit the switchbacks. Going up, Rick immediately drops back. Eric passes him, then Taylor and Barry pass him.

They crest the steep climb and roll into the long downhill. Eric notices Vance picking up the pace. His move slashes the lead pack down to three contenders as they fly down the hill and through the corridor between the screaming fans on both sides. Eric is amazed and inspired by all the people screaming—not necessarily for him, but toward him. He's still concentrating on Vance, who's moving farther and farther away. *He was right,* Eric thinks. *I'm not nervous anymore. Just excited.*

The rest of the Regal boys dash down the hill and into the corridor. They look like a sure winner, with the white eagle-emblazoned jerseys all close to one another near the front, even though Rick is still losing ground to his teammates.

Among the spectators, Paul is cheering his team on while a group of girls surround him. Mike's varsity letter jacket is a little big on him, but it does the job.

Eric wants to conserve his energy for the next hill and is swallowed by the second pack. Mike passes him, then Barry, Taylor, and Kyle are all in close attendance.

The two Hammond runners lead Vance up Poop Out Hill. Mike and five more runners go up next. A few steps back, Eric leads Barry, Taylor, Kyle and a few more boys, all starting to work hard now. Rick has fallen way back and is out of contention. Eric feels strong going up the hill, inching ahead of his competitors.

Not like last week, he thinks, *when I fell and had to go around slower runners to catch everyone.* Teammates, Kyle and Taylor are among the runners falling behind up Poop Out Hill.

The race at the front is still undecided as the three leaders pass the two-mile mark. The two Hammond runners surge on the short downhill. Vance matches strides with them, then keeps running hard on the flat, quiet backside of the course.

Mike is next to pass the two-mile marker and sees the leaders speeding up ahead. He glances back to see Eric right behind him then surges on the short downhill. Eric doesn't sprint but does widen his stride as other runners come beside him to form a second pack of twelve runners. Barry is in back of the pack; Taylor and Kyle have dropped off and are in the next group. Eric notices Rick running hard just ahead of him on the flat. Rick takes a quick glance back. Eric recognizes that look of distress: Rick's tiring. Just then, two runners push past Eric. Still feeling good, Eric responds by gradually picking up the pace and staying with them.

The leading trio come to the last big hill. Vance attacks the hill and breaks away from the two Hammond competitors. The next runner is still Mike, but now the two runners who passed Eric are right on his heels and Eric is still with them. They hit the final hill and Eric is surprised when the two runners ahead slow up. Eric maintains his momentum and swerves around them, his legs still fresh, he passes Mike, who strains to keep up. After fifty meters he lets Eric go. Coming up to the plateau, Vance has twenty meters on the two Hammond runners. The next runner, another thirty meters back, is Eric. And he's gaining.

While the excited crowd watches the race unfold up Reservoir Hill, people ask who the second Regal runner is. A man in a red team jacket turns to Maria.

"Who's that kid in fourth?" he asks.

"That's my son, Eric Hunt. Go, Eric!" she yells proudly.

Mike continues to drop back, losing five places. Barry has fallen back as well. Eric, all alone, is making up ground on the Hammond runners and very close to Vance's speed. As he reaches the plateau, he dashes the thirty meters of flat, significantly closing the gap on the Hammond runners before the last twenty meters of hill.

At the peak of Reservoir Hill, Vance's lead on the Hammond duo is widening with every stride. He floats down the final hill by himself. The two Hammond runners crest the peak and glance back to see Eric closing in. The older boys blast downhill and move away from Eric, who shifts to a new gear, using gravity, letting the hill give him more speed. Mike has dropped back a few more places as he crests the hill, but he's still only five seconds behind Eric.

Vance rounds Norton's Corner and returns to the screaming spectators as he races down the old paved airstrip, passing the start all alone, and then turns down the finish gauntlet.

A brown-haired girl beside Paul traces the letter on the jacket with her pink polished fingernail. "So, when did the doctor say you can start running again?" she asks.

"Oh, look," Paul says quickly, before too many questions arise, "My buddy Vance is winning it!"

The two Hammond runners separate by the time they reach the corner, but they've both gained ground on Eric, who can't stay with their new speed. The next pack is gaining on him as Eric turns the corner onto the airstrip, and he decides to make his final push to the finish. He holds off the pack as he chases the

Hammond runners, who are a few strides apart. Eric drives his arms harder, ignoring the pain that fills his legs and chest, and slowly draws nearer to the second Hammond runner. The fans scream wildly as they turn toward the finish. Down the Gauntlet, crowded by screaming spectators, the two Hammond runners sprint hard and hold Eric off.

Vance cruises across the finish line to win and jogs to a stop, then turns back. He watches as the two Hammond runners cross the line within a few yards of each other. Then he stares in smiling surprise as Eric strains over the last pesky little incline to reach the finish line alone in fourth place.

Six seconds later, a group of six runners stagger across the finish line just ahead of Mike. After crossing the line, Mike keeps trying to stop his borrowed watch's timer as he slows to a walk. Two seconds back, the next group of eight runners is ahead of the struggling Barry and Taylor.

Paul and the girls' team join Coach Morris at the finish chute. Mike, who's still tapping at the watch, is obviously annoyed as Paul comes over.

"Stupid thing doesn't work," he says, trying to remove it. Paul helps out, and when it's off, Mike shoves it into Paul's hands.

"Jacket worked fine," Paul replies, smiling at the brunette.

She smiles and waves at him. Mike looks at the girl, then back at Paul.

"Are you kidding me?" he says.

At the finish line, the crowd is still cheering as more runners come in. The cheering jolts Mike's attention back to the race. Barry and Taylor finish, followed by Kyle and Rick.

Coach Morris is scribbling on his clipboard, trying to calculate the score, as the team waits anxiously just beyond the chute. Everyone looks worried when an angry Barry walks up.

"What place did you get?" Mike asks.

"What's it matter?" Barry says.

"C'mon, do you know?" Mike says, irritated.

"Thirty-fifth," Barry spits out.

"That makes fifty-two points so far," Vance says.

"And still counting," adds Paul. "It's not looking too good."

"The team with the lowest total wins, right?" Eric says to Paul. "Like golf."

"Very good. Too bad you can't add," Mike wisecracks.

Coach Morris joins them. "Take it easy, everybody," he says. "Let's not get ahead of ourselves. I'm going to the official's table. The official results should be in soon."

Taylor walks up, looking sheepish, followed closely by Kyle and Rick.

"Taylor, what did you get?" Mike asks.

"Fifty-fifth. What did you guys get?"

"That's a hundred and seven," Vance says.

"I was fifty-ninth," Rick tells them.

Mike shakes his head. "We counted five guys already, Brainiac."

Coach Morris returns from the official's table, a copy of the results in his hand. He doesn't look happy. Eric sees his mom and Mr. Tate nearby, looking anxious.

"Well, we got fifth, one hundred and seven. Rockford took the last spot, fourth with ninety-nine points. We missed going to the state meet by eight points."

The team grows quiet. Rick shoves a bag of chips back into his bag, too upset to eat.

"Oh, man. We beat them at League just two weeks ago," Barry says.

"Is that it?" Rick asks.

"Yep," replies Taylor. "That's it. Season's over. Except for Vance."

No one knows what to say. Finally Coach Morris breaks the silence.

"Look, guys. We lost as a team, but I'm proud of all of you," he says, walking around the disappointed team. "Cross country can seem like an individual sport, but you've become a real team. There's a unity among you guys. You're half-milers, distance runners, and a soccer player all running together, seeing how tough you can get. Yes, Vance will go on to represent us at the State Meet, but he won't be alone. We'll all be there supporting him, I hope—and our other State Meet qualifier." Coach Morris turns toward Eric as every eye watches.

"No. Are you kidding me?" Mike says, figuring it out.

"Eric qualified. This team has two individuals going to State," Coach says, beaming at Eric.

Mike falls over as everyone congratulates Eric and Vance. Ellie hugs Eric, who's very pleasantly surprised. When she steps away, Kyle moves in to hug her but she directs him to Eric instead. Reluctantly, Kyle gives Eric an awkward hug.

"I don't believe it!" says Mike. "He's just a freshman! He's a pipsqueak. Crap, if I hadn't had a bad race, that would be *me* going to state!"

The whole group goes silent with dismay. Eric retreats, as if wanting to hide. Mike's outburst is making him feel awful on the proudest day of his life. Ellie moves next to Eric to console him and the guys take notice. She shakes her head in a negative way to oppose Mike's words. The team stares at Mike.

"Mike, go walk it off!" Coach orders. As Mike storms off, the coach pulls Vance and Eric aside.

"I know you guys run some extra stuff on your own, so whatever it is you've been doing, I want you to cut it in half. I want you to have fresh legs," Coach says.

Paul tries to keep Eric's spirits up as they walk back to the parking lot. "This is awesome," he says. "This is just what you need. The points from State are huge. You'll letter and get that varsity jacket. And, you've hacked twelve seconds off the gap between you and Bryce. You're cemented on the freshman all-time list for Mount SAC. You ran one second slower than Bryce's best! You're on the verge of passing him!"

Eric stops walking. "Paul, can you just stop? Please!" he says. "I'd rather not talk right now." He starts walking again, and Paul trails behind him silently.

Eric's dad sits eating at an empty dinner table. He finishes his sandwich and takes his plate to the sink, where Maria is washing dishes.

"It might be *nice* to see Eric run at least one cross country race," she tells him.

"Why? So I can see him embarrass himself by getting last like he did the last time?"

"He just qualified for the State Meet in Fresno."

"State Meet? Hmmm. How did he get that? Can't he just embarrass himself closer to home?"

"He's doing very well. If you'd come to any of the meets, you'd have seen how much he's improved. Remember, he made varsity and helped the team win the league championships."

"Varsity? League champs?" Dale repeats with some interest.

"This is the last race of the season," she adds.

"When is the race?"

"Next Saturday."

"Next Saturday? Can't. Even if I wanted to. I have the alumni game to go to."

"Can't you just go once? He asks for you every time."

"We'll see."

It's lunchtime at Regal High. Eric walks with his tray of food toward a group of cross country team members sitting at a table outside the cafeteria. He's just about to approach them when he sees Mike at the table. He puts his head down and turns away to an empty table. Vance takes notice of Eric and elbows Mike, and motions with his chin toward Eric. They watch Eric plop down at a table by himself and begin to eat. Vance and Mike get up and approach him.

Vance pushes Mike forward in front of Eric, "Hey, Eric, Mike has something to say to you," Vance says. Eric looks up hesitantly.

"Uh, yeah," Mike says. "You did a great job. You beat me straight up. I'm sorry about what I said." He holds out his hand. Eric takes it, surprised at the apology, gives Mike's hand a firm shake and the tension between them eases.

"Why don't you come over and join us," Vance says. Eric gets up and follows them back to their table. He notices the team is all wearing their team sweat tops except for Vance who's in his varsity jacket.

"Hey, guys. Why are you still wearing the sweats?" Eric asks.

"Cause, the season's not over yet. You and Vance have one more race," Taylor says.

"Yeah," agrees Barry. "Plus, we're league champions, man!"

Paul comes running over to meet the team.

"Hey, guys, I have some news. Another freshman made it to state. Guess who?" Paul asks.

"Bryce," Eric says.

"Correct. So two freshmen will run at State. You and Bryce," he tells them. "And he'll probably be in the top twenty-five, too," he adds. "You have to be in the top twenty-five to letter. Do that and you're a shoo-in. Get it?"

Eric looks incredulously at Paul for a moment. Eric knows the time has come to challenge Bryce. He's not sure if this is the moment he's been waiting for or the one he's been dreading. The other team members exchange glances as Eric looks worried.

Later that evening, Eric is in his bedroom, dressed in his varsity singlet and staring at the computer screen. His eyes narrow to read a running message-board post, carefully going over each screen name and what the particular writers have to say.

> **Track Star**: Bryce started running age-group track in sixth grade. This new freshman doesn't have anywhere near Bryce's experience.

Eric sits back and fidgets in his chair, thinking, *Sixth grade? Wow.*

He clicks to another page. Bryce is pictured, a slight grimace on his face, crossing a finish line. The heading reads TOP FRESHMAN. Below the picture it reads:

> **Todd Bryce.** The Skyline High freshman harrier is the number-one man on the varsity team. Bryce, the top freshman in the country, was sixth in the Mt. SAC varsity race, blazing a 15:23!

Eric picks up his log book and looks over his times.

He ran fifteen twenty-three a month ago. There's no way I can beat him.

He clicks off the computer and the screen fades to black.

"Top twenty-five," Eric says, getting into bed. He lies on his back, takes a deep breath, and lets out a sigh. "I'm in trouble."

Eric chooses a place on the grass under a tree and plops his backpack down. He takes out his history book, looks at it, and frowns. He knows he has to study for his next test. He can't fail this one, or he's off the team. He sits down and leans his head back against the tree and sets the book on the grass. He promises himself he'll study after a minute of relaxation. The sun feels good as he closes his eyes. He can't seem to convince himself to study. He's worried about the race with Bryce. The warmth of the sun embraces him. All of a sudden a shadow appears over him, blocking the sun. Eric opens his eyes and sees a shadow looming over him. Is he dreaming, or is this real? The rays of the sun are hitting the back of the girl's head, making her glow. The shadow moves to her left to a position in front of Eric, and he recognizes Ellie. Eric is mesmerized, he's seeing an angel in front of his eyes.

"Hi," Ellie says.

Eric blinks and realizes it's not a dream. "Hi."

"What are you doing? Sleeping?" Ellie asks.

"I'm having trouble studying. I should be going over my history but my mind is on the race."

Ellie leans in closer, "What's there to worry about? The fact that you've qualified is already a win. How many of those

dorks on the team have accomplished that? You earned a place at State. Come on, that's gotta mean something!"

"Yeah, I guess I'm just nervous. Maybe, even a little scared."

"What's there to be scared of? You're only racing seniors who've been recruited by the top colleges in the country." Ellie teases.

Eric looks at her, playing along. "Thanks for the encouragement."

"Don't worry about it." Ellie giggles.

"Well, at least I'm not the only freshman in the race. That guy Bryce qualified. He's good."

"Yeah?"

"I've raced him before, and he clobbered me," Eric says, getting more worried just thinking about it.

"I remember last season I thought I would lose my spot to this girl," Ellie says. "I was scared she was better."

"What did you do?"

"I beat her out for the spot."

"Yeah, well, I don't know if I can beat him. He's been running since the sixth grade."

"So what? I've got girls that just started on cheerleading and they're better than some of the girls who've been doing it four years."

"Really? So, are you saying, it doesn't matter how long you've been practicing?"

"It all depends on the person. But the newer person's probably going to improve more."

The last few words make an impact and Eric considers the thought. The idea instills confidence. "Are you coming to see the race?" Eric says, then wishes he hadn't.

"All the girls are coming. Besides, I want to see Bryce clobber you again," Ellie says playfully as she smiles at him.

Eric stands up and laughs. "Now I'm *really* nervous," he says, joking, but it's not too far from the truth. "Well, I got to get to the library and study, or else I won't get to race at all. See ya," Eric says as he bends down to pick up his books and backpack and strides towards the library.

"See you later," Ellie says and walks away.

Across the field, Mike and Barry watch the exchange.

"That lucky bastard," Mike says, envious of Eric for getting Ellie's attention. "Not only is he on varsity, he's been friends with the head cheerleader *all season*."

Friday morning, as students arrive at school, Eric and Paul stop in front of the digital ground sign. The headline reads:

CROSS COUNTRY - STATE MEET

Good luck, Vance and Eric!

"The State Meet trumps the football game! That's you up there, Eric. Your name in lights," Paul says to him. Paul turns to a freshman student walking close by, "That's Eric, that's his name on the school sign."

The first student stops. "It is? Cool, man." Two other students walk by. Paul gets their attention and they stop.

"Hey, man. That's this guy up there," Paul says, pointing to Eric.

Eric looks down, embarrassed.

The student looks at the sign, "What's cross country? Is that a sport?" he asks sarcastically.

"It's running, you doofus," Paul answers back.

A passing senior walks by, "Who cares?" he says, as he continues on. Paul dismisses him with a disdainful wave.

"C'mon, let's get to class," Eric says.

"Hey, tonight's the football game," says Paul. "Are you going?"

"Naw, I don't want to run into those jerks again."

"I can pick you up. My mom's letting my sister use the car, so she has to chauffeur me," Paul says. He can see that Eric is hesitant, so he adds, "Ellie will be there with my sister."

"Okay, I'll go," Eric says. "But only 'til the halftime show. I can walk home."

"What's the matter, have to get your beauty sleep?" Paul says.

"It's only the State Meet. I think it's worth trying to get sleep for."

It's Friday night, and the Regal High football team is playing to a packed house. Eric and Paul are sitting in the crowded bleachers. It's halftime, and the cheerleaders are in the middle of the field. Eric and Paul watch them perform a choreographed routine for the fans. Eric pays special attention to Ellie as she goes through her moves.

"Ellie's pretty good. So is your sister," Eric remarks.

"Yeah, I guess," Paul says, uninterested, accustomed to the show. Eric watches as the girls perform their routine. Paul gets up and goes down to talk to his sister. Eric stays until the routine is completed, then follows Paul.

They walk up to Ellie and Vanetta, who are taking a break near the bleachers.

"Meet us at the car right after the game. We're going to stop for ice cream," Vanetta tells Paul.

Paul elbows Eric. "Ice cream."

"Uh, I can't go," Eric blurts out.

"What? Why?" Paul asks.

"I should get to bed early. You know, for the race tomorrow."

"But this is ice cream…with Ellie," Paul whispers.

The girls go back to join the other cheerleaders on the sideline. Eric is torn, a million thoughts flash through his mind. *She invited me. But if I stay, that means I have to wait through the second half. Going out for ice cream—it's almost like a date. It will be a while until the girls get to the car, and then when they finally get to the ice cream shop, I'll have to hang out for a while. The bus to the State Meet is going to leave at 6:30 in the morning! But what a great opportunity to talk to Ellie! And she invited me. We could talk, get to know each other better. What if I run a terrible race? When will I get a chance with Ellie again? But she might not hang out with me—who am I kidding? I'm a freshman, and she's a junior, who happens to be the most popular girl in school. She might just hang out with her girlfriends—or maybe there's some older guy she likes who's going—some big football dude, probably. How would THAT feel?*

Eric looks at Ellie on the sideline. She's busy chatting with Vanetta and the other cheerleaders and doesn't look over toward him. He turns and his thoughts are interrupted when he notices that Paul is waiting for an answer.

"Well, are you staying or going? The second half's about to start," Paul says.

Eric looks back at Ellie one more time. The football team charges onto the field. The cheerleaders cheer and shake their pompoms as the players rush past.

Eric decides and turns to Paul, "I gotta go," he says.

"Okay, maybe you *should* try to get some sleep. I'll see you in the morning," Paul says.

Eric nods and walks off quickly, not looking back, while Paul goes back into the bleachers. *Stick to the plan, go to bed early and do well at the race. The State Meet is more important: I'll be racing Bryce. I'll bet he's in bed early.*

As Eric nears his house, he knows he's made the right decision, even though it was a tough one, a sacrifice. It would have been fun to go out with the group and have a chance to be around Ellie, but he's made a commitment, dedicated himself each day to practice. He's worked hard, even run with sore ankles. He's developed a routine, and he's always gone to bed early to avoid groggy mornings and dragging himself out of bed to run, not like when he'd stay up late playing video games. He's improving. His grades are up. *It's working,* he thinks as he looks up through the trees at the stars. He feels good and is proud of himself. Then he realizes that he's in the park and feels safe. The two bullies are at the game. They won't bother him again. *Man, how things have changed. When school started, I was afraid of walking through here. This was their turf. I've sure come a long way, and it's all because of the cross country team. My name's on the school sign. I'm somebody now. I'm on varsity, and I'm going to the State Meet. How many freshmen get to do that?* The walk home is refreshing.

At home, as Eric gets ready for bed, he looks at his log book one last time, reviewing his progress. He wonders what it might translate to, when his mom knocks on the door and comes in with his uniform in her hands.

"Here's your clean uniform." She sets the neatly folded clothes on top of his dresser.

"Thanks, Mom."

"So how're you doing?"

"I'm nervous. I don't know if I'll be able to fall asleep tonight."

"Nights before a big race are the worst. I could never get to sleep either but the next day, I was fine. You get to bed early every night and have the proper rest, so one nervous night won't affect you too much," she says. Eric is relieved.

"Mom, did you ever have, like, a rival?" He asks.

"Sure, I did. Mary Ann was always the favorite. She beat me and everyone else for two straight years. Before the State Meet my senior year, I was the underdog as usual. I didn't think I had a chance."

"What happened?"

"She took the lead. I stayed in contact—barely. With a half-mile to go, she still had about twenty yards on me. It didn't look like I had a chance, but I could see that she was tired. I knew it would take everything I had, but I had to try to catch her. I cut down her lead—it seemed to take forever—and with about a minute to go, I could almost touch her. Right then, she looked back. That made me think she was scared, and *I seized the opportunity*. I passed her with every bit of energy that I had, I didn't let up, and when I crossed the line, she ran into me in the finish chute. She'd been half a step back the whole time. So remember—every step counts, honey. Never let up."

"Wow, Mom—thanks. I'm going to think about that when I'm running tomorrow," Eric says. He's actually excited—not afraid—to run in the same meet that his mom won.

"Good night, honey. See you at the race," she says while tucking him in. She turns off the light and shuts the door. Eric stares at the ceiling sighs, and closes his eyes.

State

The cross country team gathers in front of the school getting ready to board the van. Eric and Vance are wearing the full team sweats. The other team members are wearing the sweat tops with casual pants. The whole team is standing near the digital ground sign, which reads:

Cross Country – State Meet

Good luck, Vance and Eric!

Coach Morris takes out a camera.

"Vance and Eric, get in front of the sign," he says.

Vance and Eric get a little praise from their teammates before they walk over to the sign. The coach takes a couple of pictures of Eric and Vance standing proudly next to the sign with their names on it.

"Okay, now the rest of the team," Coach announces. The boys rush into position and start making faces into the camera.

"Get serious," Coach orders. The boys straighten up and the coach takes two pictures and then calls out, "What are you waiting for? The season's not over. Get in the van. We have two boys with a job to do."

Everybody gets into the van.

On the way up to Fresno, Eric sits quietly looking out the window. Although he's nervous, he's also excited and happy to be with all his teammates. He's surprised that they all got up early and came out to support Vance and him. The team begins a chant in their honor.

"Let's! Go! Re-GAL! Screa-ming Ea-GLES!

Go Vance! Go Er-IC! ROCK! THIS! RACE!"

The boys add, "Take a bow!" They prod Eric and Vance to stand up, clapping and whistling. Eric and Vance stand up and take a bow to Coach's dismay.

"Sit back down, you two, before you fall over and break a leg," Coach yells. The boys all quiet down while Eric sits, trying to disguise how filled with pride he is. He looks around and smiles, and even Mike manages a smile back at him. *Man, I wouldn't have believed this could happen,* Eric thinks. *I was just another freshman—I didn't know anybody. Now, I'm a varsity runner on my way to represent the school in the biggest race of the season.*

In Fresno's Woodward Park, the conditions are almost ideal: temperature in the low sixties in an overcast and windless California sky. Twenty-five teams are there to race, with more than 400 runners warming up in the park. The teams are spread out like groups of campers in their respective staked-out territories all over the park. Coaches pace the area while their runners sit about chatting and stretching. A gradually expanding crowd gathers to watch the race. Eric looks around for Ellie and doesn't see her, but he does see his mom. Eric walks up to his mom, and she hugs him.

Flustered, Eric whispers, "Mom, there's a lot of people here," and she lets him go.

"Don't be nervous. Just do your best."

Eric and Paul stand at the end of a line of about thirty runners waiting for the Porta-John. Eric takes a moment to look around and take in all the activity. *Is this feeling more nervousness or excitement?* He thinks. Mike and Barry walk past.

"Eric, what are you doing standing in line?" says Mike. "Go behind a tree."

"That's okay, I'll wait," Eric says, casually glancing around for Ellie. Still no sign of her.

When Eric finally makes it back to the Regal encampment, it's time to warm up. He starts to stretch his legs, then Vance jogs up and joins him.

"Let's do an easy mile and then do some strides over by the start," Vance says. They jog off as the rest of their team watches.

At the starting area, Coach Morris runs up to them. "Try to get out fast the first hundred meters," he says. "You don't want to get caught in the back today."

"Okay, Coach," Vance says, and Eric nods.

"Time to check in. Good luck, boys," Coach Morris says. Finally it's time for the competitors to gather on the starting line, which stretches a full fifty meters across a large field. Two hundred and three slender, intense teenagers hop up and down, blow out big breaths that puff their cheeks, and shake out their legs and arms, ready to compete.

One by one the teams are announced. Individual qualifiers with no full teams get special mention.

"The Central Inland League and Southern Section champion from Regal High, Vance Davis," the announcer calls out.

Vance jogs out from Regal's chalk-lined starting position, waves to the cheering crowd, and returns to his spot next to Eric. They tap fists for luck. Eric looks down the long line of spectators behind a string of bright-colored plastic banners, and finally he sees Ellie. She stands with Grace and Katy in a group of Royal fans. She waves at him, and he waves back. *The pressure's on now,* he thinks. *Ellie's watching.* Eric sees his mother in the group. She has a warm, confident smile on her face. Eric nods at her. He wishes his dad were here but he knows that's impossible. He tries to remain focused. "Also from Regal High, one of only two freshmen to qualify for today's race, Eric Hunt."

Eric jogs out and waves to the cheering crowd. He's almost overwhelmed by how many fans are packed along both sides of the course. He jogs back to his spot next to Vance.

"Regal High, all the way!" Vance says as they tap fists again.

"And our second freshman qualifier, from Skyline High School, Todd Bryce," the announcer calls out. Bryce jogs out.

In the crowd, Paul says, "That's Eric's competition."

"Some competition," says Mike. "He's gonna whip Eric just like last time."

"Eric has stepped up his game," Grace answers.

"Yeah, give him a chance," Katy says.

"Skyline does have cool uniforms, though," Paul says.

"Yeah, I like the red," Grace adds.

"Are you kidding me?" says Mike. You like his *uniform*?"

"I can't help it, I notice the other uniforms. Our uniforms are still the best," Paul explains.

As Bryce jogs back to the line, he catches Eric's eyes. Eric's heart jumps, and he stares straight ahead down the course.

"Quiet on the starting line. Please listen for your final instructions," says the starter.

Eric glances up at Vance who is fixated on the course, looking straight ahead.

"Let's have a safe start. If someone falls within the first hundred meters, there will be a second gun. If that happens, please return to the starting line and we'll start again. When you finish, it's very important that you keep moving all the way through the finish chute. Please do not stop. Gentlemen, there will be two commands: Runners take your marks, and then the gun. Good luck."

The crowd goes silent. Eric tries to become both completely relaxed and completely alert at the same time. A few random shouts are all that can be heard:

"Go, Jason!"

"Come on, Bakersfield!"

"Let's go, Vance!"

The starter raises his pistol.

"Runners to your marks…"

Eric crouches quickly, and the gun fires.

The fans scream, air horns blast, and cowbells clang. Todd Bryce charges to an immediate lead next to Travis, the top runner from Leigh, while the mass of sprinting runners jockey for position as the course begins to narrow down. Eric finds himself about ten meters behind the leaders—he's almost sprinting but feels no effort—and notices that he's even with Vance. Taken aback, Eric eases off and allows Vance to move ahead. As the runners converge, Eric is hit by a few elbows. He holds his ground. Just past one hundred meters, the grass ends and the race continues on a stretch of asphalt road. Many of the spectators along the wide grass area dash away from their places and head off to other points along the course. Coach Morris momentarily hangs out with Maria as she stays at the starting area to keep a good position for seeing the finish, which will be on the same grass area. Paul and Ellie run and scramble with a big crowd that's heading toward the one-mile mark.

The course angles away from the road, and the runners race over a curb and across a small patch of grass. After 300 meters, there's some jockeying going on as the congested field splits up. A few runners jump the curb and run on the grass. Eric maintains his position on the paved road past 400 meters, at which point the course turns right. He jumps a grass corner, and then veers onto a hard-packed dirt trail. After 500 meters, the red-clad Bryce and Travis still set the pace, which is fast. They begin to pull clear of the field. Not far behind, Vance runs smoothly in the chase pack of about twenty runners. Eric is in there, too. He sees Vance move to the head of the group and makes a quick decision to hang back. *Not this soon—this is fast enough. Don't speed up.*

There is a sparse crowd yelling encouragement around the half-mile mark. Along this stretch, Bryce and Travis have broken away. They pass by, extending their lead on the chase group. Even though he's on a slight downhill, Travis looks overextended and begins to back off. Four seconds back, Vance leads the second group beside another Leigh man, two Hammond runners, and five others from various schools. Two seconds back, Eric mixes with sixteen other runners. Close behind, the thick mass of the main field follows.

Paul and Ellie reach an already congested fence-lined section of the course around the mile mark. A large digital display clock flashes: 4:25…4:26… The spectators are yelling. The whistles and cowbell clanking grow louder as the runners approach. The smooth-striding Bryce is the first runner seen.

"Bryce is a machine!" Paul shouts to Ellie as the Skyline runner comes into view. "A freshman leading the race? Eric can't beat this guy!" When Bryce races past the mile post, the clock reads 4:36. "Wow. That's really flying," Paul adds glancing back at the clock.

Four seconds later, Travis flashes past with Vance on his heels, leading a pack of eight.

"There's Eric! In the next pack," Ellie says, pointing. Paul sees him. The second pack, racing three abreast, charges through the mile in four minutes and forty-four seconds with Eric in the middle. Three seconds later, a monster pack thunders by, raising dust. After the lead runners pass by, spectators dash away, to other points on the course, to follow the race.

"It doesn't look good for Eric right now," Paul says.

Ellie looks calmly back at him. "It looked to me like he's in the top fifteen at State!"

"If they keep this up, this is going to be a very fast race," Paul says surrounded by cheering fans. Paul notices the thinning crowd. Then he says, "We should go!"

They dash off toward the two-mile mark.

As Bryce climbs a short incline, he shows signs of effort for the first time. He's working hard with his arms, staring at the ground just ahead of his feet, a tensed look on his face. His speed has slowed down, a little bit, as he passes Frog Rock. Fifty meters back, Eric is surprised to find that he still feels strong and that he can see Vance just ahead. He makes another decision not to run harder, not to try to catch Vance.

Nearing the 1.5-mile mark, Bryce tops the climb and reaches a stretch of road. The hard packed dirt hill saps more energy from him. Travis and Vance, running shoulder to shoulder, have powered up the hill and are closing the gap on Bryce along the asphalt strip. Smelling blood, the two seniors surge together, leaving their group and reeling Bryce in. From the middle of the second pack, Eric watches the lead change in front of him. Bryce is passed by Vance and Travis and immediately loses contact. Eric feels great, still in his calm rhythm. He knows he's conserved energy by deciding to stay with the pack. Still waiting, he watches Vance move away.

Two coaches wearing University of Oregon jackets are watching the race unfold.

"Well, everyone was right about Vance Davis, but I'm loving these freshmen," the assistant coach says.

The remark gets the attention of another spectator, Dale Hunt, who's standing within earshot. He's just off the path, careful not to be seen by Eric so he can surprise him later. Dale hears the word "freshmen" and looks over toward the Oregon coaches.

"I know," says the head coach. "I never follow freshmen, but Bryce is an age-group star and that Hunt kid came out of nowhere and ran the same time as Bryce at Mount SAC."

"Probably the top two freshmen in the nation, right here in the same race," says the assistant. "Of course we can't compare Mount SAC times to other courses, like Holmdel, or Detweiller, but I'd take these guys against anyone. You ever see two freshmen in the front pack at California State before?"

Dale is shocked that the Oregon coaches know who his son is, let alone that they're praising him like this.

"Nope. Make sure you send the Regal coach a brochure about our sports camp for Eric. It would be nice to have him spend a week on the campus," the head coach says.

"He's on the top of my list."

Dale stands stunned as the Oregon coaches walk to another place on the course.

The spectators line up around the two-mile mark, screaming and yelling well before the runners come into view. Coach Morris is already there, waiting for Vance and Eric.

Travis and Vance approach, racing side by side, and tear up the hill just before the two-mile mark. They simultaneously gallop past the display clock as it reads 9:37.

"Vance, stay relaxed!" Coach yells.

"Go, Vance!" Paul and Ellie try to yell over the crowd. More clanking cowbells fill the air as Vance and Travis plunge down the short down slope after the marker.

Five seconds later, the second pack appears, a cluster of eight runners. Paul can see Bryce behind them, grimacing as he crests the hill before the two-mile mark. He has lost contact with the group, three seconds behind.

"Bryce is falling back," Paul says.

"And Eric's right behind him," Ellie adds.

Bryce is in no-man's-land between two packs, the second of which is gaining on him. It is comprised of eleven runners, one of whom is Eric. He's moved to the front row of runners, five of them abreast on a wide part of the trail. The other six boys are bunched close behind. Eric still feels like he has wings on his feet. There's a slight bounce to his stride as he passes the two-mile point with the clock reading 9:48.

"Eric, you look good. Just stay relaxed!" Coach Morris yells before running toward the finish area.

As Eric races by, an open-mouthed Paul turns toward Ellie. Four seconds later, a thickening stream of competitors starts to flood the trail.

"He's doing pretty well," Ellie says.

"Yeah, you could say that! We better go to the finish," Paul yells. They push through the screaming crowd and jog past a pond to the finish area. Before the crowd arrives, they find a good spot where they can watch the finish.

Vance and Travis continue to push the pace and steadily move away from the second pack, which is starting to string out in single file.

Eric had avoided pushing the pace or making any moves—until now. With just under a mile to go in the race, he attacks the short downhill. The burst of speed does two things: it takes four of his pack with him, and it bridges the gap between them and Todd Bryce. Eric reaches Bryce's shoulder and can tell that his rival is struggling hard and looks tired for the first time. Eric can feel his own legs are getting tired, too—the surge has had a price—and he starts to worry if he has enough strength left to maintain his effort to the finish. He knows he has one more move—to a flat-out sprint—still to make. He looks past Bryce at the string of runners falling back from the leading two. At this point, Eric remembers his mother's words: *Seize the opportunity.*

With three-quarters of a mile remaining, the newly formed group of six runners remains together. They reach a small stack of logs that marks a turn, take a hard left, and head toward the "roller coaster hills" a 500 meter stretch of dirt with mild ups and downs. On the slight downhill, two senior boys from Patrick Henry and Burbank, who have been following Eric and Bryce, pass them on the outside of the path. Eric reacts almost without thinking. He leans forward slightly, letting gravity pull him, and surges past Bryce, who has taken the turn on a wider line. Their elbows bump briefly, and Bryce glances over as Eric goes by on the inside path. Eric sees the recognition on Bryce's face. The race for best freshman in California is on.

Eric keeps contact with the Burbank and Patrick Henry runners but can still hear Bryce. Eric risks a glance over his shoulder and sees the scrappy Skyline kid a yard behind him, refusing to be dropped.

In front of Eric, the Burbank man drops behind the Patrick Henry man. Burbank looks tired, and Eric feels recovered now, cruising on the tall senior's shoulder. He adjusts his rhythm, passes Burbank and lets the momentum carry him past Patrick Henry as well. Eric feels space behind him. *Have I dropped them all?* Another glance. Burbank is gone, and Bryce, fighting hard, is passing Patrick Henry. But he isn't catching Eric. Inch by inch, Eric gains ground: one stride, then two. With about a half-mile left, he has forged a five-meter lead over Bryce and holding it.

Out front, the broken-up pack of men are roughly spaced in a single file line. Just ahead of Eric is a runner from Laguna Beach High. After the roller coaster hills, the course veers left again for the final stretch to the finish. Eric sets his sights on the faltering Laguna runner, who isn't hugging the inside of the path. Eric runs the tangent, skimming the few large trees that line the bend. He passes Laguna and so do the Patrick Henry senior and Bryce. They cluster briefly around a final left turn onto the asphalt road and see the long grass field that they must cross to reach the finish.

Once on the stretch of road, Eric makes his last push for home, driving his arms like he's seen good runners do in their sprints for the line. The Patrick Henry man lets go immediately. Bryce, too, loses ground, but more slowly, his eyes still on Eric's back.

Up ahead, the electrifying moment comes when Vance and Travis fight for possession of the course. They reach the wide grass area running abreast, stride for stride, and simultaneously sprint full-out. The already screaming crowd erupts into frenzy. The two leaders remain deadlocked over the long finishing straight. About 200 meters behind them, Eric focuses on the string of runners between him and the finish: directly ahead is a Hammond High runner. Eric tries to accelerate again, hurting a lot; he has very little left to give, but he's closing on the Hammond kid.

The leaders sprint wildly toward a large banner with the word FINISH across it. Just below the banner, the large digital race clock flashing the race time is nearing fifteen minutes. Vance and Travis are inseparable. They reach the banner sprinting side by side and both dive forward, crossing the line together amid shrieks of elation and disbelief. No one knows who has won. Travis loses his balance and flounders against a red-jacketed race official, who barely keeps him on his feet. Vance staggers to a stop, turns back, and walks haltingly over to Travis. The two fall against each other, eyes squeezed nearly shut in pain and relief, each with an arm over the other's shoulder.

Behind them, the stream of runners thrash across the long grass stretch, sprinting or struggling, holding form or falling apart, as they strive for the final placings of the high school season.

Bryce lets go at a crucial time, just before the three-mile mark. The imaginary rubber band that connects the two freshman rivals breaks and they separate. Eric reaches the flat grass finishing stretch with a small gap on Bryce. Eric has nothing left except the will to reach the line, but he pulls away from the exhausted Bryce.

Staring at the finish line, Eric seems to enter a nightmare. It's only a hundred meters away, but it won't come closer. The excitement of breaking away from Bryce is gone, and he feels utterly spent. He steels himself against the real threat of collapsing. *Not now. Not after all this.* Incredibly, he's still gaining on the Hammond runner. He makes the back of the boy's red singlet the focus of his entire world as the screaming crowd nearly deafens him. He could almost touch the shirt, but he's losing control of his legs. The banner still seems frozen. A movement at Eric's left makes him turn his head slightly, and what he sees is Todd Bryce, in a full, straining sprint, passing him.

Impossible. Nothing left. No! Remember! Run hard through the line!

Bryce has used everything he has, his face a mask of pain and effort, and he passes the Hammond runner but then starts to tie up, his muscles suffused with lactic acid, with forty meters left to run. He won't give up, but his sprint has taken him only this far.

Eric edges past Hammond and gains on Bryce. He is alongside him now, and amid the wild cheering he can hear Bryce's grunting breaths. With ten meters left, Eric sees Bryce's pained expression directly beside him. With a gut-wrenching burst, he powers across the finish line a half-step ahead of Bryce, in ninth place, as the clock flashes 15:19.

Eric runs straight into the yellow-shirted back of a Loara runner who has finished eighth. He turns to see Bryce collapse full-length just past the line. Eric starts toward Bryce but is ushered briskly forward by an official who is avoiding any backup of incoming runners. Eric watches as Bryce waves off help and gets up on his own.

Drained but exhilarated, Eric makes his way through the chute. As he leaves its far end, he's instantly surrounded by a euphoric crowd of teammates and friends. Eric is surprised by how many complete strangers, many of them adults, come up to congratulate him.

Fifty meters off, Paul, Coach Morris, and Maria are making their way through the crowd.

"Whoo-hoo!" Paul says to Coach. "He's number-one freshman, top twenty-five to over-earn points to letter."

"What's that?" Coach Morris says. "'Over-earn points'?"

"Eric needed to be in the top twenty-five to get the points to letter," Paul tells him.

"Who says?"

"Uh... I calculated it."

Coach Morris shakes his head. "Not true. He comes to practice and is in good standing. All he had to do was race today."

"Oh, even better. Glad I didn't say anything."

They reach the crowd and see Eric in its center. Also on the outskirts of the group is Todd Bryce. He waits until Eric looks over and then extends a hand.

"Hey, man," Bryce says. "Good race."

Eric takes Bryce's hand and grips it securely.

"Thanks. You, too. You started out crazy fast. I never thought I'd catch you."

"Yeah," says Bryce. "I felt good. I just found myself in the lead, so I thought I should go for the win, you know? No freshman boy has ever won State."

"Well, we came pretty close, right? Top ten's pretty good against these senior dudes."

"Hey, you might think this is...weird or something, but I was following you," Bryce says.

"What do you mean?"

"On the internet... looking up race results, your times. You've really improved, man. And at Prelims, when you got knocked down? You got back up and finished. I thought that was awesome."

"Well, I guess I'll be seeing you in track season," Eric says.

"Yeah, you will," says Bryce, with a bit of a challenge in his eyes. Then he holds out a fist. "Great job, Eric."

Eric bumps Bryce's fist with his own. "Thanks, Todd. "

As Bryce walks off, Eric reflects in amazement on what's just happened. *Todd Bryce has been watching my results. And he's a nice guy.*

Vance walks up and pats him on the back, breaking the moment. The rest of the gang shows up.

"How'd you place?" asks Vance.

"Ninth," Eric says proudly.

"That's *great*," Vance says.

"Thanks. How'd you do?" Eric asks.

"I won. I didn't think I was gonna hold on, but Travis was just as trashed, so when we hit the line, it came down to who had a better lean." He leans forward in a parody of a sprinter's tensed-up, chest-thrusting finish, and everyone laughs. Eric realizes that he's almost never seen Vance smile or make a joke. "We both got the same time, fourteen-fifty," Vance adds.

"Great race, both of you," Coach Morris says.

Ellie runs up to Eric and hugs him.

"You beat Bryce! And lots of seniors! Congratulations!"

Eric grins widely. "Thank you."

"I was worried for a while there," Ellie confesses.

Paul interrupts excitedly. "Yeah, you should've heard her! She was all worried about you."

Kyle says "Awwww!" and tries to mooch a hug from Ellie, who politely declines. Then everyone notices Mike moving over toward Eric. The mood turns serious. Eric is uneasy as Mike stands in front of him. After a nerve-racking moment, Mike smiles and puts out his hand. A relieved Eric takes his hand and they shake. The team breathes easy.

"That was an incredible run," Mike says.

"Thank you," Eric answers modestly. The group is overcome by Mike's sincerity, and they all surround the two teammates, congratulating them. After a moment, Paul walks up to Eric.

"In one swoop, you beat Bryce, took him down! Fifteen-nineteen! Now *you're* on top of the freshman all-time list," Paul says. "And don't forget that varsity jacket!"

Five adult photographers descend on the group and ask to take photos of Eric and Vance. Happily obliging, they step away from the crowd as Coach Morris watches proudly. The Royal athletic director, Ed Stone, walks up to Coach Morris, who's surprised to see him and doesn't notice a distinguished gentleman standing next to Stone.

"Hi, Ed! I'm surprised to see you in Fresno," Coach Morris says.

"Ken, this is Wayne Shepard," Ed says. "Wayne, Coach Morris." As Coach shakes hands with Shepard, Ed goes on. "We had some time off this weekend, so I thought I'd check on the race. Ed's a Regal alumnus, he ran cross country a few years back."

"Pleased to see your boys do so well today," Wayne says.

Coach Morris is confused and a bit nervous, since he knows that this is cross country's last year at Regal.

"Yeah, not bad—the state champion and the top freshman," Coach says, half-expecting Ed to give him the bad news.

"I saw Vance's finish. That was really exciting," says Ed. "Our school will be very proud—Regal's first cross country state champion," Ed says. "In fact, the whole team improved this year."

"Right, league champs! Wow," Wayne says. "You guys came out of nowhere to win it. And then to qualify two kids for State? I had to come up and check it out."

"Wayne's been following the team on the internet," Ed says and takes Coach's shoulder. "Can we talk for a minute? Privately." Coach nods, fearing the bad news. They walk off a few steps and form a little triangle. Ed looks straight at Coach Morris.

"Wayne here is a member of the Rotary Club," Ed says.

Wayne goes on. "When I got in touch with Ed about how great the team was doing, he told me he was thinking of dropping cross country next season."

"Yeah…?" Coach says, looking back and forth between the two men.

"Well, let me tell you. I'm *passionate* about cross country, it gave me discipline," Wayne says. "All the values I apply to my career, and to my whole life, really, I learned running cross country."

"Wayne was a pretty good runner," says Ed. "Still is, actually. He's run twenty-seven marathons."

"Is that right?" Coach says.

"Well," says Ed, smiling, "Wayne wants to save Regal Cross Country."

"*What?*"

"He wants to donate for next season, to keep it going," Ed says matter-of-factly.

"Can't let it happen," says Wayne. "You win League, and you've got this freshman kid now? What would happen to *him* if there's no team?"

"Eric *has* had a very… positive impact on the team," Coach says, unable to think clearly.

"At the Rotary Club, we feel that cross country not only served us well in high school, but that it helps people throughout their lives. Running's one of the only sports you can compete in no matter how old you are," Wayne says. "We learned discipline, time management, valuable skill sets that helped us succeed later, too."

"I'm glad to hear this Mr. Shepard, because I feel the same way," says Coach Morris. "I've been trying to figure out how to break the bad news to the kids."

"Now, this doesn't mean there'll be a budget for the season *after* next," Ed says, "but it leaves open the opportunity that financial aid could continue. We'll have to play it season by season."

"The team's only going to get better from here," Coach says.

"Keep up the good work," Wayne says as he shakes Coach Morris's hand, then Ed shakes his hand too, and they walk off. Coach breathes a big sigh of relief and looks for his team. He can't help but smile as he turns back to watch a photographer getting ready to take Eric's picture.

"Hey, kid, could you stand in front of that backdrop with the state meet logo on it?" the photographer asks Eric. Vance happily steps aside for Eric to get his picture taken.

"His name is Eric Hunt!" Paul shouts.

"Oh, sorry," the photographer says. "Mr. Hunt, could you please step over this way a bit?" Eric does, and the photographer takes a couple of shots. "Is that H-U-N-T?"

"Yes," Eric says as the photographer writes it down. Vance and Paul hoist Eric up on their shoulders, and the photographer takes a few more photos. Eric can see his mom walking toward them. Right next to her is his dad. Eric opens his mouth in shock, and the camera's power drive whines as the moment is captured.

"Got it. Now you and Vance," the photographer says. Vance and Eric put their arms around each other's shoulders and the photographer snaps away. Eric can't stop staring at his dad.

"Very good. Now just Vance," the photographer says.

"Sure," Eric says, and he jogs past the Oregon coaches on the way to his parents, who are both beaming proudly.

"Look who I found," Maria says in fun as Eric runs up.

"Dad, you came!" Eric says, throwing his arms around both of them.

"You did great, kid," says Dale. "And there's so many people here! It's like a football game."

"Eric, that was so *exciting*!" Maria says. "I'm so proud of you."

"So am I," says Dale.

"But Dad—what about your alumni game?"

Dale puts an arm across Eric's shoulders. "I wanted to support the home team."

"Guess what!" Eric bursts out. "I'm the first freshman to varsity letter at Royal!"

"Next year, you'll win this meet," Maria says.

"Oh, Mom—it's gonna take me more than a year to do that. Hey, Dad, can I have the money to buy a letterman jacket?"

"Well…if you promise to get a big one," Dale replies. "I'm still hoping you're gonna get bigger and become a wide receiver. They have to run pretty fast, you know."

"Dad," Eric pleads.

"Just kidding, Eric," Dale says, putting his arm back around his son.

The next night, after school, Eric sits back in his chair and finishes the article in the local newspaper about the cross country team, featuring him and Vance. He reflects over the events of the last three months. He's discovered a lot about himself. He's found out that he loves to run, test his stamina, and that he can endure the pain of a long-distance race. It's been awesome to become part of a team, and he's glad just to be one of the guys—let alone to be among the best runners. He's found that although he loves to race, running isn't only about winning. He's learned a valuable lesson: that if you're serious about a sport, no matter what it is, you have to manage your time to keep up with your studies. *I've got discipline now, from running hard. I used it to study hard, too. With my extra morning runs and my strides after workouts, I think I became as good a runner as I could be.*

He has the beginnings of a philosophy that will take him much farther than the next state meet: Maintain a balance, pace yourself, seize the opportunity, and stay committed—all the way to the finish.

Eric glances one more time at the picture in the paper. He's running beside Bryce, both of them flat-out, focused straight ahead, giving everything. The caption reads:

HUNT EDGES BRYCE FOR TOP FROSH AT STATE

Big Future for Regal Star

Man, it's going to be tough to stay ahead of that guy, Eric thinks. And he starts to smile.

End